VOICES
IN THE
DARK

This is a work of fiction. Names, characters, places events and incidents are used for the Author's imagination and used fictionally.

Library of Congress Control Number: 2010924838
ISBN 10: 0982665296
ISBN 13: 978-0982665299
Cover Designed: DESIGNS BY NEESHA
Editor: Tina Nance, Chyta Curry

Printed in the United States of America

"Every family has secrets."

PROLOGUE…
Dr. Corrine Castleberry

The weekend came and went. Weatherman said the temperatures were below zero with a wind chill of minus three today. He was right. Monday had arrived with its blustery chilling subzero winds. Corrine was so tired from all the unpacking that her body wouldn't move. Laying still, staring at the ceiling not wanting to get out of her warm bed Corrine felt at peace. All she wanted to do was pull the covers back over her head and stay there forever. But that would be unfair of her. Corrine had people depending on her today. So many things to do with so little time and don't know where to begin. Her alarm went off over an hour ago and hitting the snooze button didn't help much. Another nine minutes she kept saying… another nine minutes. Corrine rolled over and glanced at her clock, seven o'clock in the morning. She couldn't keep ignoring it this time, it was time to rise and get her day started. Corrine walked out on faith last year by opening a brand new practice back in her hometown and like with every new career move comes new clients. *Dr. Corrine Castleberry,* the gold-plated plaque on the nightstand read.

It was the same plaque she had sitting on her desk in her North Carolina office. Closing those doors two years ago was in fact the best decision she ever made and at the same time, the scariest one. Though all of her degrees were still packed in boxes she was proud of all of her accomplishments.

Being a recovering alcoholic and drug abuser, Corrine promised herself that when she got clean and sober, she would return to school and finish getting the necessary credits for her Masters degree in Psychology from the A&T University and did her residency at Eastern Carolina Psychiatric Department. After ten years as the Head Psychiatrist, she decided to return home to New York, where she had unfinished business with her sisters and to finally face her past sins. Though Corrine's young daughter, Malika was unhappy with the move because of the friends she left, it was for their own good. Ever since Corrine was free of drugs, her morning ritual consisted of a positive pep talk to herself. Something inspirational, with strong, powerful words that spoke of self-determination. Corrine would always reach for her bible that was given to her by her big sister, Mae on her first year clean. She had sent it by way of their Aunt Linda when she came to visit

Corrine in North Carolina. Mae dare not travel to see her because that would mean she actually cared about Corrine and she had to face her. Opening the bible sent chills down her spine. Not because of the words but because of the inscription inside. "To my loving Sister, love Mae..." if only that were true. What a joke Corrine thought.

Corrine was the third child of four girls. Mae, Mary, herself and Jackie. Their mother died almost ten years ago and their father died in prison. Supposedly another inmate used a homemade knife and stabbed him to death when the inmate realized that Corrine's father was the man that molested his daughter.

Abused as little girls, Corrine, Mae, Mary, and Jackie were sent to live with their Aunt Linda who was their mother's only living sister after allegations of sexual abuse in the home surfaced. Allegations that tore the family apart and broke their mother's heart at the time. Yet she did nothing to protect her girls. Linda took the girls in so the courts didn't split them apart. Growing up as teenagers, Mae and Jackie would run the streets with older men and experiment with sex, alcohol, and drugs. But it was Jackie, the baby sister that introduced Corrine to cocaine and a local pimp named

Trey. It wasn't long thereafter, Corrine turned up pregnant at fourteen, then again at sixteen and on her eighteenth birthday, she was with child again. The identities of the children's fathers were never disclosed. Being a child herself it was her sisters Mae, Mary and their Aunt Linda who took care of the babies while Jackie and Corrine continued to run the streets. Mae was the oldest and the darkest of the sisters while Jackie looked Dominican, Mary and Corrine were mixed. It's rumored that Corrine's and Mary's father was a white man that their mom had an affair with while their father was away in the military. Linda had one daughter with her husband Al, Eva who was very close with Corrine. But there was a rift between Linda and Mary because Al was having an affair with Mary and eventually left Linda to be with Mary. Over the years as the girls got older, their mental state and lack of respect became worse. Unable to handle the girls and their overwhelming mental needs after her sister died and finding out that her niece Mary slept with her husband, Linda felt it best for Mary, Corrine and Jackie to leave her home. Linda didn't like the example they were setting for her daughter Eva and the situation with Mary and Al was more than she could bear.

As the years went by, each sister took on the responsibility of caring for Corrine's children. At the tender age of twenty-one, Corrine came close to death when she was found wandering the streets half naked. When Mae found her she was incoherent and lost so much weight that she was unrecognizable. Mae and Linda sent Corrine to a rehab center. After two weeks, Corrine left everyone behind including her children who never really knew their mother and relocated to North Carolina to start a new life. There she fell in love with her professor in her first year of college and four years later was blessed to have another child, Malika. Though the relationship didn't work out because Corrine never healed from her haunting past, she focused on her daughter Malika and made sure she did everything to make sure she did it right this time. But Corrine's past haunted her to the point where she relapsed with pain pills. Hiding her addiction from her new baby girl and professor boyfriend, Corrine continued to go to school high on pain pills she got from a college friend to get through her days as a new mom and a student. Eventually, it destroyed her relationship with the professor and she checked herself into rehab center to get clean at the advice of another professor when her grades dropped. It was a long hard two years before Corrine was clean and started to feel like her life mattered. With a thriving career in the field she loved, life was beginning, but her past still visited her every night in her dreams. It was at this point she decided to return to her childhood hometown and face her sins. Corrine, now forty-three packed up her daughter and headed to New York to open her own practice. It was time to fix her past and mend her relationships not only with her sisters and with her children.

"Morning mother dear. I see our clocks are in sync again." Malika walked in with fresh coffee.

"Thank you, daughter. Are you ready for your first day at the office with me this afternoon?"

"Do I have a choice?"

"Don't sass me Malika. And no you don't. Make sure everything is ready so you don't miss your bus."

"Sure why not. Don't want to miss the very first day of good ole private school."

"Malika… I pay good money for you to attend that school so stop with the smart talk and get your bus. You don't want me driving you to school do you? Or would you like to go back to the way things used to be?"

"Does that include Dad?"

"No, it doesn't. You know that. Why can't we get along? Wouldn't that be nice? I do love you, you know that don't you?"

"Yes mom. I know. I have to go okay? I'll see you at your new office at two-thirty I promise." Malika ran out so fast that she didn't give Corrine her morning kiss. Something they always did no matter what. Something Corrine never got as a child, love and affection from her mother. Reflecting when she was a child, Corrine, nor her sisters received any love from their mother. Their father did it for her. "Malika don't forget your hat and scarf from the rack! Malika? Malika?" Corrine got up and walked over to the icy window to see if she could see her daughter leaving the front step. She caught a glimpse of her scarlet scarf as she wiped the window with the palm of her hand and was relieved. Corrine thanked God for her every day. Sixteen years ago, she saved her life. The truth is Corrine was damaged as well as her sisters. Some days she's okay. And other days, well, those days are the hardest. Corrine always blamed her mother for her hard days and her sisters for her sleepless nights. The things that she and her sisters went through as kids she wouldn't wish on her worst enemy. The abuse, the lies, and the secrets…all things taught by their parents when they were little girls to keep quiet. Things you never tell and secrets that you take to your grave. It's those deep dark secrets Corrine left behind that she came back to face. Corrine wished she could turn back the clock and redo her life. She wished she never had the sisters she had, but she does. She wanted so bad to tell her daughter the truth but was in fear of rejection. In fact, she hopes she never finds out the truth. Corrine prayed every day that her past sins would be open for forgiveness. Forgiveness that was thirty years in the making and in order to be free of her sins, she had to come back home. Often times she kept her mind pure of positive thoughts. Corrine fought hard for this peaceful mind and youthful body yet inside she knew something was still off. She couldn't put her finger on it. Maybe it was the daily night tremors she would have that would wake her out of her sleep like clockwork, two-thirty in the morning; this was her nightly ritual every night. And every night she tried to focus on the dream. Trying her best to give her nightmare a face. No such luck. She even tried to talk to her oldest sister about it one night. A conversation she plays over and over in her mind because Mae never answered her questions instead she talked to Corrine with such distain in her voice. Corrine hung up the phone and they never spoke of it again. But as Corrine religiously played that conversation over and over in her head again, tears began to stream down her face. She never understood why her sisters hated her so much, but she had every reason to hate them for what they did to her growing up. Especially Jackie. Corrine had so many unanswered questions from her childhood that it was like book pages being flipped really fast in her mind, but the pages were blank. It was up to her to fill in the words. But Corrine needed help. She can't continue to hide these feelings and emotions that sometimes seem to have a mind of their own.

Corrine called her assistant, Yvonne to let her know she was running late. Yvonne does the morning shift until Malika gets there. "Hey, it's me. Who is my first client this morning?"

"Brenda. But she's not here yet so you're safe. Shall I reschedule?"

"No. I'm sure she's on her way. Send her a text to remind her. If she arrives before me keep her there. I'm on my way."

"Okay."

"Thanks, Yvonne…"

Chapter 1
Brenda.

She always had to have the last word, no matter what. At an early age, her mother taught her that every child should honor the Ten Commandments. *In those commandments, it states to 'Honor thy father and thy mother,' right? But where in the hell does it say to torture thy daughter,* Brenda thought to herself.

I can't believe it! She managed to avoid me as a little girl and now even as a grown woman, she refuses to acknowledge something did, in fact, happen to me as a young girl. My mother was right about Aunt Linda. She had her own drama, not garbage to deal with. I can't believe she would think of her own niece, her own sister's daughter as "garbage". Brenda fumed as she paced back and forth, looking at her phone until she finally threw it against the wall.

Brenda's great aunt Linda, her mother's aunt, found out her daughter, Eva tested positive for HIV. She didn't say if it was full blown AIDS, but the results alone were devastating enough. Brenda could only imagine what Eva must be going through, not to mention her Aunt Linda. She wasn't about to add to her troubles, but she still believed that deep down inside, she knew something about what happened to Brenda in her childhood. Brenda sat quietly at the edge of her bed and started to cry.

The tears flowing relentlessly down her face as if someone broke her heart in two with a hammer. The crying became routine for her every night after her dreams, only this time, her own mother had made it worse. Brenda couldn't understand what she didn't want her to know or what she was hiding from her. Every time she tried to bring up anything about her childhood, Brenda's mother made it seem as though it was top secret. She made her feel she didn't have the right to ask her about anything, especially anything that had to do with her mother's parenting skills.

Brenda's mother always made her feel like they were competition with one another like they were sisters and not mother and daughter. It didn't make any sense, but it was the best way she could explain her mother's constant distaste. Mothers and daughters don't compete; they love and embrace one another. They learn from each other. At least that's what Brenda wanted with her mother, but she knew deep down inside that no matter how bad she wanted it, it was unlikely to happen.

After Brenda's mother hung up the phone, Brenda decided to make sure she had her things prepared for the morning, which would be upon her in a few hours. She was still upset; so she decided to make some chamomile tea, take a nice hot bubble bath try to relax. Brenda's home was too quiet, so she put on one of her favorite CDs, 'Kemistry' by Kem, to set the mood.

She knew she needed to call her mother back she forgot to ask her if she had the fifty-dollars she borrowed from her the week before. Brenda dared not tell her it was her last, but it was and now she needed it for gas in the morning. Brenda tried to calm her nerves down before she made that call.

Brenda stared back at herself in the bathroom mirror as the warm water filled the tub. She felt like her reflection… sad and confused. Her eyes were blood shot red from all the crying, her nose looked like Rudolph the red nosed reindeer, but she was not going to let her mother get the best of her. She allowed her to do that all these years and it was time that she took back control of her life. Tomorrow, Brenda was going to start her day on a positive note and with a positive attitude.

Damn, this feels good, Brenda thought as she slipped into the nice, warm bubble bath. "Now if I could find a man who felt as good as this bath, soothing, warm, quiet and gentle, then I would really be happy." she said as she smiled to herself. Before Brenda knew it, an hour had slipped by and she was still in the bath.

"I forgot about my tea! I'm sure it's cold by now." Brenda thought as she rushed out of the tub, reheated her tea and prepared to make the dreaded phone call.

She knew she would hear it when she called her mother back. She hated the fact that she had to ask for the money back that she had lent her mother, but she really needed it to get through the week. Her children were all grown and had their own families to take care of. She helped out here and there and did what she could.

Here she was, a grown ass woman who stood on her own two feet ever since she started working and she had to ask her own mother to return the money she lent to her. Brenda felt ashamed and worthless, but she had no choice. She couldn't ask her ex-husband because he lost all of his money gambling amongst other things that he was into. I mean, she said she would give it back to me and all I had to do was ask her when I needed it. But I know what that was about; she needed to feel in control of my life, even if it meant borrowing my money. This job is going to set me straight. *I wouldn't have to worry about any more financial issues again ask for help from anyone,* Brenda thought to herself.

As she finished her tea, she noticed the clock said nine-thirty. Even though it was late, Brenda attempted to call her mother back. This would surely piss her off...

"Ma, I'm so sorry to call you back this late. I'm starting my new job tomorrow and you said when I needed that fifty dollars back you borrowed last week to ask you. So I'm asking now if I can come by in the morning to get it from you. Is that okay?" Brenda asked. Brenda could always count on her mother to say something rude and obnoxious that would cut her deep. She hadn't failed her yet.

"For starters, I don't even know why you are wasting your time with this new position. You should've stayed in the warehouse like all the other black folks. You too good to do warehouse work, is that what it is? Sounds like a really stupid move, if you ask me. So now you need the money back tomorrow morning?" Brenda's mother replied.

I didn't ask you for your opinion about my job, Brenda wanted to say, but she knew that kind of response would've been followed up with a slap across the face when she finally saw her mother.

Brenda took a deep breath before responding. "Ma, it would mean I will no longer have to work long hours on machines anymore. My health is not that great these days. I will have my own little office and a company car. It means a lot of learning new things and growing with the company. Can't you be happy for me? Can't you at least be proud of me for once? What does this new position have to do with me asking for the money I lent you last week?" Brenda said as she let out a long sigh. Brenda finally felt like she was sticking up for herself.

"It has nothing to do with it, but it sounds like you need to contact that ex-husband of yours I don't have it to give back. Even if I did have it to give, how dare you ask me for the money back? You owe me bitch. Bye!"

Brenda knew she meant every single word of what she said. It wasn't that she didn't have it, but she was punishing Brenda for something in her mind. She was always punishing her. Brenda wanted so much to believe that somewhere deep within, her mother actually cared about her, even a little bit.

Brenda could not ask her ex-husband for anything she knew he would make her feel ten times worse than her own mother did. Brenda used to think they were tag teaming her because when they got together, nothing she ever did was right or good enough. It was possible that she fell in love with her husband who was also her childhood sweetheart because he had some traits like her mother and because she never really had a relationship with her father. What relationship she did have with her father was with his belt to her butt most of the time. Brenda's father was a military man apparently like her grandfather and he traveled a lot. He would often be stationed in different places, but he always sent her mother money to take care of her and her sister.

Rumor has it that Brenda's mother squandered the money on men and liquor. At the age of eleven, Brenda overheard an argument between them one night. He doubted that she was his child. Her dad stood six feet tall with a deep voice similar to that of Barry White. He was of a dark complexion with a salt and pepper low fade. When her father spoke, one couldn't help but stand at attention. No one ever wanted to test him and the ones that did usually ended up being very sorry.

Brenda's parents divorced when she was fifteen and her mother started seeing George, a big time Investment Broker back in the day whom she later married. George was whom she came to know as the father figure in her life, her stepfather. He was very handsome with a swagger similar to that of Denzel Washington. He was charming and had it together.

Every chance he got, he spoiled Brenda's mother and she loved every minute of it. But George was also a hustler on the side, loved the ladies and made his big money slanging' in the streets. Some say that George had a deep; dark past that no one talks about and will never speak about. As soon as the money started rolling in any love that Brenda's mother did have went right out the window. Brenda never knew how to love another person like they should because her mother never really loved her since she was a child.

So here she is, living alone and ready to move on with her life. Somewhere in the midst of her failed marriage, emotionally abusive mother, seeing a therapist now these dreams… there was still something holding her back and preventing her from moving forward. Brenda had been in therapy now for six months with two other women. According to her psychiatrist, Miss Castleberry, her story was an extreme case she should be doing everything in her power to resolve any issues Brenda may have with her mother. *She may be right, but something has to give and at some point I will find out the truth.* Brenda vowed.

VOICES IN THE DARK

Chapter 2
Brenda's Tragedy...

It was the morning of her first day on her new and job and Brenda finally mustered up what little strength she had to herself together. Brenda may be thirty, but she didn't look a day over twenty-five. Her blue jeans fit right; her black shoe-boots coordinated well with her black cashmere turtleneck sweater, 'cause ole man winter was not playing outside. Brenda never wore a lot of jewelry, only her diamond cross, two gold bracelets from her cousin Eva and her diamond ring that she bought herself almost five years ago to celebrate her divorce. Her hair was nicely wrapped thanks to the hottest hairdresser on the planet, Miss Kim! Brenda's nails along with her feet were freshly manicured. Brenda had never really pampered herself until her cousin treated her to a spa salon for her birthday a year ago.

Brenda walked over to the mirror that hung right outside of her closet door and thought, *Yes, I must say, I'm looking damn good for my first day as a supervisor.* If only Brenda's mind and heart could catch up with her look, then maybe she would feel better about herself. She grabbed her keys, locked up the house headed out the front door. She prayed all the way to her car that she would make it to work on the little gas she had.

As Brenda headed down the stairs to the front of her brownstone, old man winter slapped her dead in her face. The snow was thick and made it hard to see even a few feet ahead. She took a glance around her block and saw her little car about ten feet to the right of her brownstone.

"Good Morning, Miss Brenda, how are you this fine morning? The man whose name she never knew greeted her.

He was always outside when she left for work. She couldn't tell if he was waiting specifically for her if he loved to be outside this time of morning.

Brenda was always polite with a quick, "Morning," and kept it moving. He seemed like a nice man, but he still gave her the creeps. He wore the same dirty, green trench coat every day. His light brown construction pants were so dirty it looked like he had been rolling around in a can of oil for years. They always sagged, which exposed his disgusting belly. His boots were covered in soot, unlaced the tongues flapped over the boots. The community she lived in nicknamed him Dirty Harry he resembled an old dingy washed up Clint Eastwood, except he was the black version.

"Morning, have a good day." Brenda said as she hurried past him without giving any real eye contact. She wanted to be polite without being rude or downright nasty.

"You sure do look good today you have a good day as well. Stay warm in this weather." Harry yelled back with a devilish grin, showing his stained, brownish teeth as if he was proud of them.

"Thank you," Brenda said as she sprinted to her car to get out of the cold.

Brenda quickly opened the door and slammed it behind her. She had taken her keys out of her purse and said a hail mary to herself that her car would start. When it was bad weather, her car took almost fifteen to thirty minutes to get completely warmed up. Brenda swore she would get a new car as soon as she had more money coming in. Her old Toyota Corolla was about to meet his fate with the local junkyard.

"Come on baby, don't fail momma this morning," Brenda said to her car as she started the ignition. Brenda took off her black leather gloves and rubbed her hands together to keep them warm. That's when she got a call from her Aunt Linda on her cell phone.

"Brenda, it's Auntie Linda, how are you doing this morning, baby? Your mother told me you called her last night."

One thing about Brenda's mother was that she could never keep her mouth shut about her personal business, especially if it was negative. She loved to run and tell it. But if Brenda were doing well, her mother wouldn't utter one word to anyone about any of Brenda's accomplishments.

"Hi, Auntie, I'm okay, except for these dreams I keep having and Momma always avoids my questions. She told me not to bother you, so I'm a little shocked that she called you." Brenda said.

"I don't know, baby, but you know your mother, she answers to no one. Sometimes I wonder if we are really blood-related, but don't tell her that." Linda said. They both let out a snicker because if Brenda's mother heard them, she probably would never speak to either of them again.

Brenda's Aunt Linda let out a long sigh and said, "I was calling you about your cousin, Eva. She really needs your support now. I can't believe my baby may go before me. I hate to bother you with this first thing in the morning."

"It's okay, Auntie. I was going to call Eva after work today and maybe ask her to go to dinner with me. I can't go into much detail right now because I am trying to get to work and I'm already running late." Brenda said.

As Brenda's car started to warm up, she saw dirty Harry coming closer to her side view mirror by the driver's side. She knew who it was because of that dirty trench coat he wore.

"Auntie, can you hold on for one second?" Brenda asked her Aunt as she rolled down her window to see what he wanted.

It was the biggest mistake of Brenda's life. Before she could get the window more than halfway down, he smashed the glass and punched Brenda in her jaw. The blow to the jaw was so strong that blood flew from her mouth and she went across into the passenger seat of her car. Before she knew it, he had forced his way into her car.

Brenda never did hang up from her aunt. She could hear her from the phone. "Brenda, you okay? What's going on? Brenda, what's wrong? Answer me, Brenda!" Her aunt screamed through the phone.

Brenda heard her auntie's voice but she couldn't move nor respond. She was paralyzed with fear and powerless. All she remembered was Harry's foul breath all over her. His disgusting, long wet tongue licked the blood off her face as if he was a hungry bloodhound looking for food. Harry was too big to fight off. His body was well built, yet he had a potbelly as if beer drinking was his only hobby. His face was rough and unshaven.

Brenda screamed with fear. "Don't do this! Please don't do this, Harry!" The tears flowed down Brenda's face like a waterfall.

With his Swiss Army knife in one hand held up to her throat, Harry motioned her to be quiet or else. He then unzipped his foul, dirty brown pants, pulled out his erect manhood and teased Brenda as he began to stroke himself in front of her, forcing her to watch. He tried to force it into her mouth. Brenda pleaded and shook her head no.

"Please don't make me do this, is it money you want? Please, no!" she begged.

Harry punched her again. "Shut up bitch and do what I said!"

Dirty Harry leaned back in the driver's seat as a bloody Brenda gave in to his demand. The snow was coming through the broken glass and piling up on Brenda's head.

With every gag and choke from Brenda, Harry shoved his manhood harder and harder into Brenda's throat. "Yeah, like that, bitch. And stop all that damn crying, you know you want it!"

It was early in the morning and the snow was so thick that you couldn't hear a dog howl from miles away, so Brenda's tormented cries went unheard. Harry then took the pocketknife and grabbed the back of Brenda's neck lifting her up telling her to take off her pants. When she wouldn't, he slashed her belt buckle and unsnapped her pants. He then motioned for Brenda to get in the back seat.

In fear of what he might do, she climbed in the back seat wearing nothing but her bloody coat and scarf. Harry jumped all over Brenda's cold body. Brenda tried to wiggle her way out from under him, but there was little room in the backseat of the car. She was pinned down with nowhere to go.

Harry took the belt and wrapped it around Brenda's throat and tightened it with the loops. "Shut up bitch!"

He then pulled on the belt tighter and tighter which almost cut off Brenda's oxygen. Brenda tried to block the belt with her fingers so she could breathe, but Harry slashed her knuckles.

Harry forced his way inside Brenda's tight vaginal walls with thrusts so forceful she tore. Harry was stronger than her and overpowering. He kept slapping her over and over again with an open fist. Every slap Harry landed, matched each thrust, ripping Brenda's insides even worse.

Brenda could feel her vagina go numb as Harry did his business. She was so overcome with pain, that she fixed her eyes on the brown and black torn hole in the ceiling of her car where she had burnt it with a cigarette from a party one night. Harry pumped so fast and so hard, her legs and inner thighs felt like they were on fire even though it was freezing outside. The faster Harry went the more and numb she became.

"You pretty bitch! I'll show you how to acknowledge me in the morning! You like that bitch? Say you like it! Say you fucking like this dick!" Dirty Harry grunted and groaned as he reached pleasure in causing Brenda pain.

With no lubrication, he pounded her tender vagina until it was raw causing lacerations and bruises. Harry spit a glob of dirty, green phlegm in her face, then took his knife and slashed Brenda's cheeks giving her a lasting memory of the nightmare.

"Say you like it! Damn bitch, this pussy feels good! I knew you would be sweet!"

There was obviously no foreplay and he was someone she didn't care for nor desired as a man. His hot breath became labored as he approached climax. The fact that she resisted him aroused him even more. The more she fought, the more he felt her vagina tighten around his throbbing manhood. Brenda couldn't believe what was happening to her. She wanted to scream for help, but her body went numb. Her legs became limp and she was beaten until she was powerless.

Why is he doing this to me? Brenda thought. She could still hear her auntie screaming for her from her cell phone, which had flown to the floor, but she couldn't reach it to answer her. Her cut up knuckles were in so much pain, she couldn't extend her hands to reach her phone. Brenda had no voice to speak. With two sharp thrusts, he ejaculated his rotten semen inside her and collapsed on top of her in satisfaction.

Harry laughingly zipped up his pants and was gone, leaving a bruised, sweaty and beaten Brenda lying there helpless. Finally, the ordeal was over, but the consequences were about to begin. All Brenda could feel was the cold wintery breeze across her bruised body and cut up face. The snow from the storm started to fill the inside of the car as the icicles covered Brenda's wounds.

Brenda blacked out; hearing her auntie say, "Hold on baby, the police are on the way…"

VOICES IN THE DARK

Chapter 3
Traci...

As Traci was driving to work in her green '87 Honda Accord, she thought to herself, *Dammit! I'm running late again! I don't know if I can take too much more of this madness. It's now starting to affect my own life I can't have that. But what was I to do? She is my mother and she gave me life. I couldn't let her fall. I couldn't stand for that to happen to her again this time, it would all fall on me.*

Traci's mother was arrested a few weeks ago for prostitution and they found cocaine on her. She had solicited to an undercover cop and then tried to sell him a rock. The worst of it was that she had, Dominique, Traci's baby sister with her. Since Traci wasn't her sister's legal guardian yet, they called Trey to get her. Trey was her stepfather, as well as a pimp and a drug dealer. Calling him wasn't making anything better; it made her mother's situation worse.

Trey paid her bail and she was released from jail with a date to appear in court within a few weeks. Traci never knew how she always got off from the charges against her, but rumor had it that Trey had some cops on his street payroll. When the court got wind of Trey's criminal record as well as his past problems with cocaine they put Dominique in a temporary foster home until her mother appeared before the judge. The judge was a black woman herself. She looked to be in her forties maybe or she may be in her early fifties. When her court date came up, the judge's verdict stayed embedded in Traci's head.

"Traci, are you willing to take sole custody and full responsibility of your sister, Dominique until your mother is well with and with a stable home? It will be up to you to care for her and provide her with a home and lots of love." The judge said it with such conviction in her voice.

Traci responded, "Yes, your honor, I am willing and ready. My family needs me I want to help in any way I can."

Traci could tell the judge was a little taken aback by her response because of the way she looked at her. It almost seemed as if she wasn't sure of the decision she was about to make. She looked at Traci with nurturing, loving eyes. A look that Traci wished her own mother would give to her. Then she spoke to her with such tenderness Traci will never forget it.

The judge looked down at her folder, closed it and said, "Well that's very admirable of you, Traci, but remember you can't keep helping someone that doesn't want to be helped. Please take that into consideration. I hope through all of this, you find a support system for yourself. You may be seated."

As Traci went to sit down, she glanced around the courtroom to see if her mother had made it in. She was always late to her hearings. About five minutes after the judge's statement to Traci, her mother finally arrived. Traci knew her mother was high on something when she walked in the courtroom. She looked a hot mess and she smelled of booze and weed.

Traci had to quickly pull her mother back with her hand if she got any closer to the judge, the decision could've been far worse than what it was. Even Traci's therapist, Miss Castleberry came to show some moral support, but her mother never noticed. That is when the judge asked her mother to rise.

"Miss Johnson, in all my years of being a judge, I've never been more disgusted with a case than what I've read in your file. You don't deserve to be a mother and I don't say that lightly. Yet, it amazes me how you half raised such a well-rounded daughter in Traci. You have been arrested for prostitution, sale of cocaine to an undercover officer, assault suspected abuse of a child. The mere sight of you disturbs me and leaves me no choice but to give you the maximum sentence that I can hand down by law. But, I know that will not help you or your children. They say rehabilitation is key in situations like this; however, I am a little leery as to if it will work for you. I see standing before me a beautiful young woman, willing to stand up and take responsibility for her sister and her mother, fully knowing her mother's drug habits." Traci's mother wasn't even looking at the judge as she was speaking then the judge glanced over at Traci.

"Traci, the court admires your strength in taking responsibility for your family, but the court also understands you have a full thriving life to live. I would hate to see it go downhill because of your mother and her shortcomings." She then directed her decision to Traci's mother.

"So, it is the court's decision that since your daughter is willing to take responsibility to release you, Miss Johnson to the care of your daughter, Traci. You are also to report to Moore Counseling Foundation four times a week, as well as meet with a court-appointed probation officer at the end of each week. You will go over your counseling sessions with the officer. I am also ordering that Dominique is not to be around Trey until the court establishes paternity. Miss Johnson, this will be your responsibility to have this happen. I applaud the efforts of your daughter, Traci to handle this situation, but make no mistake about this decision, if you're arrested again for as much as a traffic violation, you will do hard time and I will show no mercy with the sentence. Do you understand what the court has decided today, Miss Johnson?" The judge stood up and looked down at Traci's mother in disgust waiting for a response.

Her mother stood there motionless. Traci was praying so hard that the judge didn't smell her or worse; asks her mother to step forward.

"Miss Johnson, do you understand the ruling of the court?" The judge started to get very impatient, but her mother managed to get out a half believable response to the judge's ruling.

"Yes, your highness." Miss Johnson said in a stuttered yet sarcastic tone.

"Excuse me, Miss Johnson, what did you say?" The judge was not amused by Miss Johnson's response.

"I said, yes your honor. I understand." Traci's mother looked as if she was about to fall down, but she managed to stay up.

"Court is adjourned. Traci, the court wishes you luck... next case."

As soon as court was over, Traci's mother tried to prove to her that she wasn't high, but she knew better. She used to buy the drugs for her mother. Her mother always had this glassy look in her eyes when she was high. They were blood shot red, but she always managed to hide them with big black shades. She would quickly have an attitude about everything and towards everyone when she was high on something.

"Traci, baby, let me talk to you for a second," her mother said as she stumbled past the courtroom doors, running after Traci. She grabbed her arm and spoke to her in a low tone, but that was her mother's way.

"Ma, what the fuck do you want?" Traci snapped at her mother because she was so disgusted by her attitude in court. Her mother didn't care about anything or anyone but herself. Traci stood there, staring at her mother with the disgust on her face. "You heard the judge. But then again, you only hear what you want to hear, isn't that right, Ma? I really don't have anything to say to you. You really out did yourself this time, showing up high and drunk. How could you?" Traci asked her mother.

Traci's mother punched her in the mouth like she was a man. "Bitch, let's not forget who is the mother and who's the child! Now when you pick up Dominique from them people's house, bring her to her momma, so I can take her out to eat."

Traci's mother always thought that taking Nique, who was her youngest daughter and Traci's baby sister, out to eat would make up for her behavior. Their mother always assumed that since Nique was only six years old, she didn't know any better that she would get over her being arrested. Little did she know, Dominique hated it and told Traci all the time about how mad and sad she was at their mom for shat she did. Even though Traci's mother would rarely hit them, she still had this way of making them feel unloved by talking down to them. Their mother was good at it. Deep down inside, she didn't mean it at least that's what Traci wanted to believe. She was high when her high came down, she would quickly apologize.

Her favorite sympathy game to play was being very apologetic after she did her wrong. She wanted people to always feel sorry for her and it usually worked. But Traci, being her daughter, knew better. She was cold and manipulating and when she was high she acted as if she was better than almighty God himself. Even at the age of twenty-three, Traci dare not raise her hand to hit her mother back. She couldn't bring herself to do it. No matter how evil her mother was towards her, she was still Traci's mother. Traci still gave her that respect as her daughter.

"Jackie! There was no need to hit her! She's your daughter and in reality, she's all you got left. I really don't think you want to do this here, do you?" Corrine was at the courthouse to support Traci and that is when she witnessed the entire exchange between Traci and her mother as she was coming out the courtroom. Her mother hated Corrine because she felt that she was trying to take her place as Traci's mom.

"This is my motherfucking daughter, bitch! She's mine! Not yours! I raised her! Stop trying to be something you and I both know you can never be! Now if you don't mind, miss high and mighty, my daughter and I were talking." Miss Johnson said with a snotty tone as she pushed Miss Castleberry out of the way and tried to finish talking to Traci, but Traci wasn't trying to continue the conversation. Watching her mother embarrass herself was making her sick.

"Ma, there was no need for that. I will pick up Nique and bring her to you. Go home and stay there. I will call you when I'm on my way." Traci said.

"That's momma's baby!" Her mother gave Miss Castleberry a look of death and brushed past her as of to confirm her statement that she was indeed Traci's mother.

Corrine was not moved by Traci's mother's actions at all. In her profession, she came across people like this all the time. Corrine handed Traci a tissue from her purse. "Traci, I'm sorry your mother is treating you like this I wish I could do more for her. She really does need a lot of help. But as the saying goes, you can't save someone who doesn't want to be saved, right? Do you think she will take heed to the judge's words?"

As Traci wiped the blood from her bottom lip where her mother had backhanded her, she looked at Miss Castleberry with one tear in her eye. Her mother had appeared in front of several judges she never followed their recommendations.

"No, Miss. Castleberry, she won't, but that's my momma. Who else will look out for her if I don't? If you don't mind me asking you, what did my mother mean by you and her both know you couldn't? Did I miss something?" Traci asked

Corrine lifted her chin, looked Traci dead in her eyes said, "Traci sweetheart, who will look out for you? Something you need to think about. Your mother is high, so I wouldn't worry too much about what she said. She probably doesn't even know what she said meant either. I'll see you in therapy on Friday. Call me if you need me."

"Thanks, Miss Castleberry, I will." At that moment, Traci realized she was all-alone on the stairs of the courthouse. She never forgot that day...that was six weeks ago.

VOICES IN THE DARK

Chapter 4
Traci's family values...

Two weeks had gone by since
Jackie's court appearance but nothing had
changed in her life. She was still doing
drugs and putting her children in harms
way. "Ma, calm down. I'm on my way to you
now. Have Nique ready when I get there."
Traci said to her mother in an angry, yet
concerned tone.

"Traci, Nique isn't here, she's with
her father. He showed up unexpectedly this
morning and insisted he take her to school
so I let him. I didn't really see any harm in
that. How far away are you?" Traci's mother
sounded like a smoothed out jazz musician
high off weed.

"Are you crazy!" Traci shouted at the
top of her lungs. Traci looked down at her
cell phone because she couldn't believe that
her mother was up to her old tricks again.
She knew damn well he was coming over
and Traci bet her life that he was there from
the night before. "Ma, if I didn't know any
better, I'd swear you were trying to
purposely lose custody of Dominique to the
court system. You know Trey isn't supposed
to be around her and definitely is not
allowed to take her to school! You better

hope and pray that the school doesn't call your case worker." Traci said.

"Traci, I really don't need this bullshit from you right now! He's Dominique's father and yours too for that matter. It really doesn't matter how pissed off you are at Trey or me! Keep your commentary to yourself and bring me my damn medicine." her mother screamed at her.

Traci knew damn well that her mother was not to allow her sister to be with Trey. It was a court order! Paternity hadn't even been established yet and she was back to her bullshit antics. As Traci headed to her mother's house, she couldn't help but remember how good things used to be. They were happy as a family at one point. As she thought even harder, that's the last time any of them were truly happy, especially her mother. It wasn't until she linked up with Trey when Traci was seven years old and he got her mother hooked on drugs. Cocaine was her favorite drug of choice; then came crack. That is when everything went downhill and fast!

Traci' never really knew her real dad because he left her mom when she was three years old and she tried to make it on her own. That's when Trey came into the picture and he began to pawn Traci off as his daughter. Her mother even went so far as to change Traci's name from Linae to a name that sounded like his first name. But what could she do? Traci was shy of her fourth birthday at the time and her opinion didn't matter. Trey was a pimp and a well-known drug dealer. He was known around town as "Big T". Whatever you needed or needed done, he was the man to see. But even Trey had a boss to answer to.

Growing up, Traci, her mom and Trey all lived in the local housing projects on the South side of town. South City Towers was eight tall, brick, broken down buildings that almost reached the sky, complete with five floors with five apartments on each floor. It was nicknamed "high city projects" because the good drugs were in South City. It was once said that Trey had no moral conviction to his hustling. Trey was into everything, from prostitution to drugs to extortion and some even accused him of murder and child pornography. Trey was tall, smooth cocoa-brown complexion with Indian features. He stood six foot three with jet-black curly wavy hair; hazel brown eyes with deep dimples the cleanest smile you have ever seen. He was so fly and always dressed with the latest fashions from Coogi to Armani. He never wore the same thing twice.

Every woman wanted Trey, but his heart only belonged to one woman and that was Traci's mother, Jackie. Everyone would always say Traci favored her father who Traci never really remembered; but Traci felt it was strange that she looked nothing like her mother, no resemblance at all except maybe in the cheekbones. It was something that haunted her daily, but she never questioned her mother about it. Her mom used to be well known in the community because she owned her own beauty salon in town called Mi-Ma's Salon. She did everyone's hair and pretty much employed anyone and everyone who needed a job within the community.

The worst mistake of Jackie's career in the hair business was to employ the hood. People would always steal from her, sometimes even when they were getting their hair done. She had her own car, paid her own bills, but she still wasn't happy. When it came to Traci, even as a little girl, she had no love for her. She would always remind Traci of how difficult her life was becoming, due to having her. Her favorite line was, Traci, if it wasn't for you, I could have this man. Or, what am I going to do with you because I need to handle some business? Why are you always in the damn way?

Trey made her mom his main woman. He would buy her anything she wanted get her high leaving Traci behind with a friend of hers. Somehow, in spite of her mother's selfish ways and neglect, Traci still managed to set goals and work toward them. Traci wanted to be a nurse. She graduated South City High with honors and enrolled in the local college for her LPN. Two years after she graduated high school, her mother lost her beauty shop. The police raided it and found three kilos of cocaine stashed in the storage room where she kept her products. Jackie knew it belonged to Trey, but she took the fall for him anyway.

When Traci entered her first year of college, her mother gave birth her little sister, Dominique. Now that Traci is in graduate school with only a year left and has started her internship with Havana Medical Center, all Traci wanted to do was to give Dominique a stable home with lots of love and support.

Traci arrived at her mother's house and once again, her mother was high as a kite. She was standing on her porch with a cigarette in one hand and a Heineken in the other. Traci was used to seeing her this way all the time. This was the normal morning routine for her.

"Hey, Ma, how are you? I still can't believe you allowed Trey to take Nique." Traci said while her mother stared at her with one eyebrow raised and rolled her eyes.

Traci handed her mother her medicine and pulled up a chair next to her on the front stoop of her house. "I can't keep doing this for you, Ma. I could lose my internship at the hospital behind this." Traci said in a disappointed tone.

Her mother could care less. She was once a very beautiful woman, but the streets had really done a number on her, along with Trey's helping hand. Her hair was now a dirty salt and pepper grey. Her once thick Coca-Cola bottle frame was now as thin as a toothpick and she looked anorexic.

"Thanks, Traci! You know how to be careful sweetie. Momma taught you well so don't worry your pretty little head so much." her mother said.

She was right about that! She taught Traci how to pick pocket at twelve and she always resented her mother for that.

"Thanks a lot, Ma! I mean don't you care at all if I get caught? Do you even know how much I am risking for you? This is my career you're talking about, not to mention my freedom." Traci said.

"What career, Traci, you won't last long. You will drop out like I did. When will you give up this stupid dream of being a nurse? It's almost laughable. I'm nothing, so you're nothing. Like mother like daughter. It's in your genes girl." She snatched the brown bag from Traci's hand and looked inside to make sure she didn't forget anything.

Traci gave her a kiss and a hug goodbye. She had to get to class before the professor asked her once again why she was late. At this point, she was running out of excuses.

"Ma, I have to run. I'll see you when I get off work."

Traci kept it short and sweet because if she argued back with her on what she said, they would be fighting in the streets. She had no time for that today. As Traci went to give her mother a hug, she turned around, looked up and there he was! She tried to keep her composure and keep walking, but he stopped her within inches of her car.

"Well, will you look at what we have here? Hey Traci! You looking good baby girl and you smell so sweet!" Trey said as he had grabbed her arm to stop her from getting into her car.

"Let go of my arm, Trey! You may have my mother fooled, but not me! Not by a long shot! I suggest you let go of my arm!" Traci said, as she made sure they locked eyes.

He knew Traci wasn't playing around.

"Oh c'mon, Traci, baby, we both know how you feel about me, your daddy. Do I need to refresh your memory?" Trey said.

"You are not my daddy, Trey! You are not even a man! My memory is fine. I remember what you tried to do to me as a little girl. Shall I tell my mother right now?" Traci laughed as she stood up to him then slapped him with everything she had in her. She wanted him to feel her rage.

"That was to refresh your memory of that night! You could never be the man my daddy was! Don't you ever grab me again or I promise you it will be the last movement you ever make! Don't try me, Trey, I'm not my mother!"

Trey stood in amazement, holding his jaw with the look of death in his eyes. Traci knew she would have to pay for that later.

He had nothing to say to her so he let her arm go. She left him standing there staring at the back of her tires as she sped off. Traci knew in her heart that she and Trey would bump heads again. It was only a matter of time.

Chapter 5
Shalae...

At about three o'clock in the morning, he walked in as if nothing was wrong. Shalae could tell he had been drinking and smoking weed all night. He had a stench that she could smell from the couch as he stumbled past her and into their bathroom to wash up. He only washed up when he came in after being with another woman. He didn't even notice that she was half-asleep on the couch. Shalae wanted to say something, but the doctor told her that she had to remain stress-free in her first trimester.

"What's up, She? I know you aren't sleep. Get the hell up and make me something to eat." Brian always demanded that she fix him something to eat when he came in. That's because after smoking blunts all night, he had the munchies.

"What's the matter? Your other chick couldn't handle fixing you something to eat?" Shalae said, not missing a beat to Brian's comment. One thing about Shalae, her mouth was as sharp as her suits that she would wear to work. She was always getting slick by the mouth, mainly because she knew it would piss him off.

"What did you say to me? Don't you ever speak to me like that again! Now get me my food! Crazy bitch!"

Brian, with an open hand, slapped her right across the face for her sarcastic response, sending Shalae clear across the living room floor. He made sure he always left a mark on her to remind her that he was in charge. Shalae should've expected that he was drunk and he would always hit her when she didn't move fast enough to serve him. But this time, she was going to give him exactly what he wanted and deserved.

"I'm going! But the next time you hit me like that, it will be your last!" Shalae yelled as she got up from the floor and ran to the bathroom to see her bruised face.

Brian yelled from the living room, "Yeah, whatever She! How many times have you said that to me? I'm losing count! Go fix your face and get my food. Hurry the fuck up. A nigga is starving." Brian said as he plunged into the cream leather couch Shalae bought a few weeks ago with her bonus check.

Shalae walked past Brian and into the kitchen to heat up the spaghetti she had made the night before. But this time, she was going to add a little something extra to show Brian that she wasn't playing his games anymore. She was tired of the beatings, the fighting she was running out of excuses at work as to why her eyes were always bruised and swollen. Shalae added some grated cheese on top of the spaghetti along with some other extra sharp ingredients.

"She! She! Don't make me come in there after you, girl! Hurry up!" Brian yelled.

"I'm coming, dammit!" Shalae shouted from the kitchen.

As Shalae walked over to the couch, Brian was comfortable in his red and black Hanes boxers, watching the big fifty-four inch TV that she had bought. Shalae dare not even try to change the channel because that would result in a never-ending battle with Brian's fist in her face. It was already four am she had to be gone by six am to get to work on time. Shalae knew that after Brian ate his food, her morning would be a long one, but she didn't care. Shalae was tired of the bullshit and she had had enough.

"Here you go, baby. I'm sorry I took so long to heat it up. But here you go your drink too. I am going to go to bed; you know I have to be up in a little while. I love you." Shalae said with a devilish grin on her face as she walked back to their bedroom.

"Yeah…yeah…go ahead man, I'll be in there when I'm done. You better be ready too."

Shalae knew that once he was finished eating, he would try to have violent sex with her, but she made sure that this time it wouldn't happen. As Shalae listened to Brian devour the spaghetti, she lay still in her bed waiting to hear the screams, but they never came. She peeked out the bedroom door to look at him through the living room mirror. He hadn't touched his drink yet. What was he waiting for? He always went for the drink immediately after he finished his food. That was his routine. Why was he changing up his routine now?

At that moment, her cell went off. "Hey Shalae, it's your wake up call. Time to rise and shine, it is five am and you don't want to be late." The automated lady said on the other end as Shalae answered the phone.

Shalae hated that morning wake up call, but her mother, Mary, had set it up for her, so she could keep tabs on her. Shalae had an alarm clock to wake her up; she didn't need the extra wake up call. It was time to go to work, no time left for any sleep. She had to meet with her new supervisor early, so she went into the bathroom to fix her face. Somehow, Shalae mustered up enough energy to get out of bed, shower, put on her favorite interview suit then some flat shoes. Even though she was a few weeks along, her clothes had started to feel a little snug her feet had started hurting a month prior to her finding out that she was pregnant. She wore comfortable sneakers, but packed her shoes in a separate gym bag in case.

As she headed toward the living room and past the couch, the TV was still playing loudly. He had fallen asleep, which meant he never touched his drink. Shalae decided to leave it right there on the coffee table. At some point, he will touch it and will know that she means business. Too bad she wouldn't be there to hear the screams.

Like any other normal morning, she would always try really hard to wake him up and kiss him goodbye. It never worked. He was always drunk from the night before and he never knew what hit him. Shalae grabbed the keys to his truck off the coffee table, locked the door behind her headed downstairs. At some point today, Shalae knew she would get a phone call from him or someone else.

As she headed to work, she kept thinking about her mom and when she would go through this routine when she was a little girl. Her dad would beat her mom daily for no reason at all. She thought Shalae never knew what was going on, but she did. Her mother, Mary would always look up at her from the floor with her fingers over her mouth and whisper, "Shhh." She didn't want him to come after her daughter.

Shalae was very afraid of her dad growing up. When he got drunk all hell would break loose. Shalae's mom would try so hard not to get beaten, but when she would cook dinner, she would get smacked for not answering a question loud enough or looking at her dad the wrong way. Shalae's dad had a real serious problem, but her mother loved him. Shalae never understood why she stayed, but now that she is in that same position, she understood the fear. Shalae was petrified of her fiancé, Brian. She didn't have it in her to leave him. They did have some good times, but more bad than good. Shalae always thought to herself, *one day he is going to kill me*... then what would her momma or her unborn child do without her?

"Come on, move your damn car already. People need to get to work!" Shalae hated taking this way to work. Traffic was always heavy at this time of morning on the bridge heading towards the inner parts of downtown Manhattan, but it was the only route to get to her job in time. Her job was only twenty-five minutes away from her house, but it seemed like it was hours the way people drove in the morning. As Shalae arrived at work and was walking through the parking lot, her mother called her as she did every morning.

"Shalae, baby are you sure you are alright? Did you make it to work alright?"

"Yes, Momma, I did. I am okay. How are you doing? How is your arm?"

Shalae heard from her aunt Linda that her dad had broken her mother's arm a few days ago. Her mother never tells Shalae these things because she knows Shalae would chastise her as if Shalae didn't have her own life to worry about with Brian. Shalae always found out what was really going on with her mother and father from her aunt because Shalae would always have to talk her aunt out of killing her father with her bare hands.

"I take it your Auntie called you? She never minds her business! Well, I am fine and well… you know your father. He doesn't mean it. He has a lot on his mind." Shalae's mother said.

"Momma, they never mean it. They always have something on their mind. It usually ends with them beating us. I'm sick of it, but I fixed Brian's ass this morning. He should be feeling my wrath in a few hours when he wakes up." Shalae said as she chuckled devilishly to herself.

"Shalae! What did you do? Why would you go and get Brian angry? Why are you starting trouble?"

"Momma! I'm not the one starting the trouble! I'm sick of fixing my face with all kinds of makeup before I head into work. My boss knows and so do the people I work with. I'm tired of making up excuses. I don't even like makeup!"

"But Shalae, you know Brian will come after you. Like your father did with me. It's not worth it baby, it's not! Why don't you go see that nice lady that you've been talking to lately? What is her name? Miss C. something…"

"Momma, please let me do this. I will be fine. After today, Brian will no longer test me. Mark my words, he won't. I have to head into work. I will call you when I get out. Plus, Ms. C. doesn't see me until Friday after work. She is helping, Momma, she is. I'll talk to you later, love you."

As Shalae approached work, she was excited, yet terrified to walk through the doors.

VOICES IN THE DARK

Chapter 6
Shalae's Escape…

Shalae walked into work and couldn't help but notice everyone staring at her. It was as if they saw a ghost. She walked as fast as she could to the elevator and to her luck no one got on with her. She had no idea what that was all about, but it was creepy. Shalae worked in a big communications building and had to go to the fourth floor to get to her office. She sold medical instruments to hospitals, doctors, medical colleges, universities and some research centers. Shalae loved her job and some of the people she worked with. They were like her fairytale family that she always dreamed of, but today seemed like she was stepping into guarded territory.

"Hey, Shalae girl, how are you doing?" Yvette was always so giddy in the morning.

"Yvette, I could ask you the same thing. What's going on around here? I walked into the lobby downstairs and everyone was staring at me. What is going on, did I miss something?" Yvette stood up and gave Shalae her makeup mirror from her desk.

"Yeah girl, you forgot to put on your shades this morning. You know no makeup can hide what Brian did to you. Girl, when are you going to leave him?" Yvette asked.

"You mean that's why everyone was staring at me?" Shalae had this pretend dumb look on her face as if she didn't know that was the reason, but deep down she knew.

"Girl, have you seen your face? Look at it in the mirror. He jacked you up good, I see. What was the reason this time? You didn't move fast enough up the stairs or something? Girl, I don't know how you can still live with him."

"I love him, Yvette! I mean it's not as bad as it seems. Brian is really a good person. I'm working on leaving him; I need a little more time. I do believe after today, he won't be hitting me ever again." Shalae shouted at Yvette without really raising her voice. She didn't want the whole office to hear their conversation.

"Shalae! That man doesn't love you, but his fist sure loves the hell out of your face! I mean c'mon, you yourself said you watched your mother go through hell at the hands of your own father, so why would you put yourself in that position? Have you even told Brian about the baby yet? What if he hurts you so bad you lose the baby? Have you thought about that?" Yvette said as she folded her arms in anger and turned her chair around.

Yvette was coming on strong, but Shalae knew it was because she cared about her and the baby. She didn't want to see anything happen to Shalae. What she didn't know was that Shalae had really planned on leaving Brian as soon as she saved up enough money to be okay. Shalae was stashing a few dollars away in a shoebox, as well as a separate safe that he had no idea about. A tip that Ms. C told her to do for herself in case she decided to leave because with money in bank accounts he would find her.

"Yvette, I am going to tell him about the baby tonight over dinner. Let me borrow some of your foundation, I left mine at home."

"Shalae, nothing is gonna help that black and blue eye of yours. You need to find some shades to put on. You know you have to meet with the new supervisor today about your position. How are going to meet her with that eye? I will go find you some."

Yvette was right, Shalae needed to leave him, but she needed to get a little revenge before she did that. Her plan was all set too. Nothing was going to stop her this time.

Yvette finally made it back with some tinted glasses. Shalae looked at Yvette with one eyebrow lifted and said, "Girl, who do these shades belong to?"

With her mouth twisted to the side and eyes rolling, Yvette said, "Does it matter? They look like reading glasses so just put them on your face girl At least you will look professional when you talk to the big lady. Are you excited? I am so happy for you, girl! This is what you needed to get a fresh start. Now, let's cover up that eye."

"Yvette, you know how I feel about makeup. I don't need it." Against her own judgment, Shalae took the makeup.

"Girl, if you don't fix that eye of yours, you'll need a new job. Now fix your face because there goes Miss Peterson now."

As Yvette applied the MAC foundation, Shalae stood up to check herself in the big mirror on her desk. That's when she saw the big boss lady walking down the hallway, coming to get her for the hiring interview. This interview was to make sure she still wanted the position, which was a supervisory role, as well as sign some paperwork and get her financial forms in order. New position meant new money, which could result in a new location.

"Shalae Smith? My name is Miss Peterson and I am your hiring interviewer. Are you ready to go to the next level?"

"Yes, I am!"

"Glad to hear it. Follow me, Shalae," Miss Peterson said as she headed down the hallway to the conference room.

"Good luck, girl!" Yvette whispered as Shalae left the cubicle with a pen and notepad and followed Miss Peterson to the end of the hallway.

Shalae was on her way to a new beginning and she was very excited. The whole interviewing process took about two hours. There was plenty of paperwork to fill out, videos to watch hands to shake. As Shalae was about to shake the VP's hand, Miss Peterson came over to her very nervously.

Miss Peterson gently grabbed Shalae by her hand and pulled her off to the side from the meeting. "Shalae, you have an emergency call at the front desk. You can take it over in that office in the corner to give you some privacy."

"Thank you, Miss Peterson."

"Oh, call me Janice. You're one of us now. I hope everything is all right. Keep me posted. Walk through those brown doors and turn left."

"Thanks, Janice, I will. I'm sure everything is alright."

As Shalae headed through the brown double doors, her heart started to beat faster and faster because she knew she would be getting a call. Shalae knew it would be Brian crying like the little bitch he is. He wouldn't have the nerve to call the police after all the things she knew about him, but Shalae wanted her revenge and this would be it. She saw the phone off the hook, but her body was too nervous to pick it up. She was really afraid of what was at the end of the line. Would it be Brian or the police? Only one way to find out… Shalae picked up the phone.

"Shalae Smith?"

"Yes, this is Shalae Smith and who is this?"

The voice on the other end sounded concerned, yet calm, almost nurturing. "This is Nurse Meadows over at the County Hospital. There is a young man named Brian who was brought in by ambulance. He says you're his wife. Are you his wife?"

"No, but go on." Shalae really wasn't interested in what the nurse had to say. She was tired of the beatings.

"Well, somehow he swallowed several pieces of glass and he is in critical condition. Would you happen to know who did this to him?"

"Yeah, maybe... Is he going to live?" Shalae questioned because she wanted to be sure of the validity of the nurse's concerned tone. She didn't think she left that much in the sauce.

"Well yes, he will recover, but he won't be able to speak. Can you come down here? He really needs to have someone here with him."

"Yeah, I guess when I'm done I will try to make it, but don't count on it. I will see what I can do." Shalae could tell the nurse was as shocked at her response as she was, but this made Shalae feel powerful and safe.

As Shalae walked back to the meeting, Janice approached her with yet another issue. This time, her power would be taken out of her like that.

"Shalae, I don't know how to say this, but the police are here to see you. Does this have something to do with that phone call?"

"Janice, I hope not. Let me find out what they want. I'll be right back. Don't worry, everything is okay."

Shalae met the policemen as they walked down the hallway, but when they finally reached her, she was not prepared for the news they gave her at all.

VOICES IN THE DARK

Chapter 7
Hospital visit...

Brenda's cousin Eva arrived at the hospital, insisting on knowing the whereabouts of her cousin. Eva is very demanding like Brenda's mother because Eva's mother and Brenda's grandmother mother were sisters. "Hi, my name is Eva, a relative of mine was brought into the trauma ward earlier this morning. May I see her?" Eva said as she stormed over the nurse's station.

The nurse asked, "Who is your relative, sweetie?"

"Her name is Brenda, Brenda Johnson. She's sort of my cousin." Eva said angrily.

"But I thought her mother was called that she was coming for her. I don't know if I can let you see her before her mother gets here the police." The nurse said as she moved the clipboard from Eva's reach.

"It was my mother, Brenda's great aunt that was on the phone with her when this was taking place. I suggest you let me see her or you and this hospital will have a huge problem on your hands. Now let me see my damn cousin. Don't feed me that policy bullshit!"

"I could lose my job!" The nurse started to get an attitude with Eva, but she was not backing down. They went back and forth for a few minutes until the police and the hospital security showed up.

"Ladies! Ladies! Please, this is a hospital for sick people. Keep it down. Now what seems to be the problem here?" the detective asked.

"Well, Officer, this nurse won't let me see my cousin. She was attacked this morning and brought in. I was able to get here she won't let me see her." The officer took Eva aside as his partner began to question the nurse.

"I'm sorry, what is your name?" he asked.

"My name is Eva. Why can't I see my cousin? She needs to be with family right now, after what happened to her."

The Detective took Eva aside. "Eva, I'm Detective Mills that's my partner Detective Raynar. It was our understanding that we were meeting with her mother to try and get some information from her about Brenda. Do you know where she is? We really need to talk to her."

"Her mother isn't coming, nor does she care what happens to Brenda. I am here for her, so you ask me whatever you want.

My mother is her great Aunt. Now when are you going to let me see my cousin?"

Meanwhile, Detective Raynar had begun collecting information from the EMTs that came in the ambulance with Brenda earlier that morning.

" I can't let anyone into the rooms because they say they are related to the victim. I am not about to lose my job. The last time we did that, some girl stabbed her husband. Our policy is strict, especially when the patient is as bad off as Brenda." the nurse told Raynar.

"So she was beaten pretty badly?" Raynar asked.

One of the EMTs put her hand on Raynar's shoulder and leaned in to speak softly. "Her face is pretty messed up she won't speak. I think she is more in shock than anything else. If that woman Eva is really her cousin, then she will need her."

"Where were we? I need all you have on her condition, so I can put it in my report." Raynar said.

"Yes sir, I sure hope they catch the monster that did this to her."

"We will, don't worry, we will. There will be police patrolling that area."

The nurse went back to her station to gather the information to give to Raynar.

Eva was still trying to plead with detective Mills to let her see Brenda. After getting the information he needed for the investigation, he persuaded the nurse to let her in to see Brenda.

Eva walked into Brenda's room and was shocked. Brenda lay still in the hospital bed, motionless. Cuts and bruised covered her arms and fingers. Her face looked like Mike Tyson himself had pounded on her for twelve complete rounds, nonstop. She was unrecognizable. Her front teeth were missing she had black and blue bruises with dried up blood covering her bottom lip. Brenda was facing the window with a blank stare.

Eva pulled up a chair next to Brenda's bed, and held her hand to comfort her. "Brenda... Brenda, it's me, Eva."

"Eva, please explain to me why he do this to me?" Brenda didn't want her cousin to see her like this. She didn't want anyone to see her like this. She was so ashamed felt like this was all her fault.

"Oh sweetie, I don't know. Do you know who did this to you? Brenda, I am so very sorry this happened to you."

Brenda shook her head no. "Eva, where is my mother? She was supposed to be here. I told the nurse to call her and tell her what happened to me. Is she outside?"

Eva smiled and held Brenda's hand as her eyes started to water. Brenda could not tell by the look on Eva's face that her mother wasn't there, nor was she coming.

"Brenda, your mother isn't coming. You know it like I know it. I didn't want to say anything I know you want her to be here for you." Eva said reluctantly.

"Eva, I know, but I was hoping. Even now in my worst crisis ever, she still won't come." Brenda turned her face and gazed out her room window.

"Brenda, I can't believe this happened in your neighborhood. It seemed to be so quiet over there. Did he... well... you know..."

"Did he rape me? Is that what you mean, Eva? Is that what you're asking me, Eva? Do you want to know all the gory details? Where would you like for me to begin?" Angry tears fell as Brenda answered.

"Brenda, I didn't mean to upset you. I only wanted to know what happened. We don't have to talk about it. I can sit here and hold your hand. In fact, why don't I get something for us to eat, sound good?" At that moment, both detectives entered

Brenda's room ready to question her about what happened. She didn't want to answer any questions. She wanted to erase this memory from her mind like she did everything else. She wanted to forget this ever happened.

"Brenda Johnson? I'm Detective Mills and this is Detective Raynar we need to ask you some questions about this morning."

Eva got up from her chair to give the detectives time to speak with Brenda. "Brenda, I'll get you something to eat and be right back. Excuse me detectives don't get her too upset. She's been through enough already."

Brenda turned her face from the officers and said, "Officers, I have nothing to say to you. I didn't see his face I don't know who did it."

"Miss Johnson, the nurse this morning said you were pretty clear on who did this to you. If you're afraid, we can protect you."

"Detective Mills, no one has ever protected me before, so what makes you any different?"

Meanwhile, on the other side of the hospital...

"Excuse me, ma'am, are you family?" The nurse asked as she tended to Brian's IV drip.

"Well, according to the patient, I'm his wife. How is he?" Shalae responded.

"Well, he can't speak right now, but he will be able to in a couple of months. I am so sorry about what happened to your husband, this was such a brutal crime."

It was no crime, Shalae thought to herself. Brian got exactly what he deserved. Shalae told him she had had enough this time she would get her point across. She was tired, especially tired of being beaten. Shalae looked at him. He looked so innocent lying there in that hospital bed, but they both knew that was so not the case. Shalae stood over him and they looked at each other as if they both wanted to kill.

"So, they say you can't speak, but can you at least nod your head?" Shalae whispered in Brian's ear.

Brian nodded, but he was also balling up his fist on the side of the bed. As soon as the nurse left the room, Brian grabbed Shalae by her shirt collar and pulled her down towards his face. He was so angry with her that he wanted to punch her in the face, but he was in so much pain, He could only manage to get enough power to shove Shalae to the ground.

Shalae immediately stood up and smacked him across the face. Even in the hospital bed, he was still abusing her. Brian wanted her to feel like he was still stronger than she was, but Shalae wasn't about to give him that satisfaction.

Shalae leaned over Brian's bed and said, "You think you can't speak now? Do you really want to keep testing me, Brian? Next time, I will make it so you can't walk! I'm tired of you beating me. This time, you don't get to win. You call me your wife, when you don't even know how to love me! Haven't you had enough already?"

Brian stared at Shalae with his lips turned up. She could tell that all he wanted to do was call her names make her feel the way he always did, which was less of a woman. But he was in too much pain to continue fighting with her. He attempted to get out the bed to get at her, but he fell. The nurses rushed in to help him up. Even though Shalae loved this man, she hated him for what he did to her at the same time. She couldn't help but to feel sorry for him. He was in such pain it was starting to wear her down.

One of the nurses glanced over at Shalae, as if to say help us, but she couldn't. It was as if Shalae was frozen in time and couldn't move. She wanted to help him, but for the first time since her and Brian been together she felt like she was in control. Like she had the upper hand and dammit, it felt good. At that moment, Shalae remembered the other reason why she was at the hospital.

"Are you going to just stand there or you're going to help us?" one of the nurses said to her in a very nasty and arrogant tone.

Shalae walked over to them and helped them lift Brian off the floor. Shalae still didn't feel sorry for putting him in the hospital. One way or anther, the hitting had to stop. Once they got him back in the bed and into a comfortable position, Shalae noticed the look in his eyes. He gave the same look that he had given her during all the previous beatings. The look that said he wanted to kill her.

He tugged at one of the nurses to hand him the pen and paper from his nightstand. She reached for it and handed it to him. The whole time that Brian was writing, his eyes were fixed on Shalae. He couldn't speak, so he used the pen and paper to express himself when he needed to talk. This was the suggestion of the therapists who came to see him before Shalae arrived. The nurse took the paper from Brian as he nodded his head in Shalae's direction signaling to the nurse to give it to her.

Shalae looked at the paper it read... *This isn't over, bitch!*

Even with his tongue half gone, he was still being Brian. Shalae knew at that very moment her fight would never be over. Shalae looked at him, crumbled up the paper, threw it at him walked out. He could lay there and die for all she cared. As Shalae stormed out of his room to let him know she meant business, she bumped into Miss C, who wondered what she was doing there.

"Hi, Miss Castleberry, what are you doing here?" Shalae asked.

"Hi, Shalae, I came to see a friend who was admitted earlier, but I guess she's doing fine. Are you okay Shalae? You look a little stressed out. Come sit down with me. How is everything with you and Brian?" Said Miss C with a confused look on her face.

"Everything is fine, Miss C. well, sort of fine. He's here in the hospital, which is why I am here, but I really don't want to

talk about this with you right now. I have to
see my mother… apparently she was
brought here as well."

"Oh, Shalae I'm sorry to hear that.
What happened to her?"

"My father is what happened to her,
Miss C… my father is what happened. , I
have to run, we'll talk this Friday in
therapy."

"I hope so Shalae…"

Chapter 8
Miss C...

"Miss C, there is a young lady on line one for you." Miss C's secretary walked in right behind her as she dropped her bags by the door.

Miss C turned around to her secretary said, "Can you take a message? I'm about to have a session and can't be interrupted."

"She said it's urgent. The first thing I did was offer take a message, but she said she had to speak to you now." Her secretary said as she rolled her eyes up to the ceiling.

"Do you know who it is?" Miss C asked.

"She said her name was Brenda that you were supposed to see her this morning."

"But... I... put her through...Tell my client I will be right with them." As her secretary walked back out to the lobby, Brenda rushed right into the office and sat down.

"Breeeenda, hi, how are you doing?" a startled Miss C asked as she wasn't expecting her to call.

"I'm not doing so well, why didn't you show up at the hospital?" Brenda responded as she wiped the sweat from her forehead while talking to Miss C.

"Brenda, I did, don't you remember?"

"I think I would remember if I saw you, Miss C. It doesn't matter, they're releasing me in a few days, so I don't think I will make it to therapy for a while. Maybe I need to stop coming altogether." Brenda expressed exhaustedly.

"Brenda, I completely understand, but I don't think we should stop now. Plus, you never told me exactly what happened to you. I think we should talk about it." Miss C wanted to continue, but she could tell Brenda wasn't in the mood.

"I don't want to talk about this to anyone, not even you. Why should I? So you can analyze me and try to figure me out?" Brenda became increasingly agitated with Miss C and her continuous effort to push her.

"No, Brenda, so we can get to the bottom of things. I think what's happening to you is very normal, however, I also feel that you're trying to resolve things the wrong way. We can get this under control if you continue the sessions, please don't stop now Brenda we are so close to your breakthrough."

"I don't know, Miss C.; I will see how I feel in a few days when they release me. I will call you and let you know."

The last thing Corrine wanted was for Brenda to stop her sessions. Doing so could mean a dangerous outcome for her. They had come so far she was sure that Brenda could handle it. Maybe if she reached out to Brenda's mother found out where her head is at, it may help Brenda... then again, it may not. That was a meeting she wished to avoid if possible.

Corrine signaled for her secretary to let her client come in. "Malika, you can bring my client in now."

"No problem, Ms. C but is everything okay with that woman on the phone? She sounded so desperate to speak with you."

"Yes, everything is okay. Hold my calls for an hour send in Mr. Clark."

A frail, old, dark-skinned man came walking into Miss C's office. He was dealing with the loss of his wife.

"I'm sorry to have kept you waiting, Mr. Clark, but I had a very important phone call to take that needed my immediate attention. So let's get started, shall we?"

As they started his session, Corrine couldn't get out of her head how Brenda thought that she didn't see her today at the hospital.

Chapter 9
The Ward...

"You're late again, Traci. I can't keep covering for you like this. What was it this time or was it that no good mother of yours," her friend Carmen said handing Traci a clipboard and a pen.

"Carmen, I don't need to hear no shit from you today. No, it was not my mother." Traci snapped back.

"Uh huh, you say that all the time. That no good mother of yours is going to cost you your job. Is that what you want? Anyway, you know who came by here looking for you today. I swear Traci, when are you going start creating a life of your own and stop taking care of that needy family of yours. You know they don't care about you, the few dollars you drop off." Carmen grabbed Traci's arm so they could do their rounds.

"Carmen to me, they are my family and I will be there for them for as long as they need me, end of story. Now can we please make these rounds? Oh, for the record, I have no time for a love life, before you ask that question again." Traci said rolling her eyes.

Carmen sucked her teeth and threw another clipboard at Traci as they headed down the hall, checking each room to make sure the patients had what they needed. Traci needed to give Carmen the slip, so she could grab some more medicine for her mother. She gave her mother all she could get, but her mother wanted more.

"Carmen, I need to go to the ladies room. How about I meet you in ten to get coffee from downstairs?"

"That's fine Traci but don't have me waiting forever like you did last time."

"I won't. I promise."

Traci had to make it quick, it was time for her supervisor to come in and she was always on time to check up on them. She could not risk getting caught; she would lose everything. Traci swore this would be the last time, but as she said that to herself, she remembered saying the exact same thing the last time she did this for her mother. As soon as she approached the cabinet she saw her supervisor.

"How are you doing today Traci?" She never even looked up at her. Every time Traci's supervisor greeted her, it was always with her face down in her planner.

"I'm fine Miss Drake." Traci mumbled.

"If you are okay, then why are you standing by the medicine supplies and not making your rounds with Carmen like you're scheduled to do? This ward in the hospital doesn't pay you to guard the supplies. Is there something you need?"

"No Miss Drake I came by because Mr. Paul needed his insulin. I saw on his chart that no one had given it to him." Miss Drake looked up at Traci and looked dead in her eyes. She knew Traci was lying, but didn't say anything.

"See to it that Mr. Paul gets his insulin and catch up to Carmen with your duties and report to me before you go home this evening, okay Traci?"

"Yes, ma'am."

Traci could tell she was on to her. She had stolen from that same medicine cabinet too many times for the hospital or Miss Drake not to notice. "Dammit, Momma... I may lose my damn job over this then what will I do?" Traci whispered to herself.

Traci headed downstairs to the cafeteria when she saw Trey. *What the hell was he doing at the hospital?* She decided to be nosey and follow him to find out what he was doing there. As Trey headed down the hall, he went up to the Nurse's station and then walked into one of the rooms. Traci went right behind him without him seeing her. She walked over to the nurse's station to find out whose room he's visiting.

"Tanya, who was Trey coming to see?"

"Now Traci, you know I can't tell you that. Why don't you ask him yourself?" Tanya, who was one of her college friends, worked the second floor of the ward.

"Because he and I don't get along you know why! Stop playing with me, Tanya."

"Well, you didn't hear this from me, but rumor has it the guy in room 213 is a witness against Trey for one of his cases he has pending." Tanya whispered.

"And you let Trey walk in and see him? Trey could kill that man! Tanya, you have no idea what Trey is capable of!" Traci said.

"Yes I do, Traci. I know, but he also threatened me, and my son if I didn't tell him what room. You won't tell anyone will you?"

"Tanya, you better hope nothing happens to that man tonight on your watch. I got to go before Warden Drake catches me."

"You are too funny, girl! Thank you so much, Traci. I owe you."

"Don't worry about it, Tanya. I know how threatening Trey can be, but hopefully soon all of that will change…"

All day, while Carmen and Traci did their rounds, Traci was terrified about what Miss Drake wanted to see her about.

Whatever it was, she was prepared for it.

Chapter 10
Session One

Even though the hospital released her Brenda didn't want to go to the therapy sessions with Miss C anymore. Brenda knew she would make her talk about the incident. It had been two days Brenda didn't want to talk about it with anyone.

"Hi, Malika, can you tell her I am here?"

"Hey, Brenda, how are you? I'm so sorry to hear what happened to you. If you need an ear, I think I'm close enough that I would hope you call on me if you need to." Malika said.

Brenda smiled. "Thanks, Malika I will if I need to. I see that girl, Traci, has arrived as well. I sure hope her session is after mine."

"Uh, I think so Brenda. I will tell Corinne you're here."

"You'll tell who?" Brenda had a confused look on her face.

"Corinne, Miss Castleberry. I will tell her that you're here."

"You know, Malika, in all the months she's been counseling me, I never knew her first name."

"Oh I'm sorry. I probably shouldn't have said that. Our little secret, okay, Brenda?" Malika said with a smile.

"You got it, Malika."

Brenda wasn't too sure about this other girl that the doctor was seeing. She was a young, very pretty girl, but seemed to have an arrogant way about her. Every time Brenda had a meeting, so did she. They always locked eyes Brenda could tell she wanted to ask her something but it never happened. Brenda said hi to her maybe once or twice, but she sits there in silence.

"Brenda, Miss Castleberry will be right with you," Malika said as she sat down at her desk outside Miss Castleberry's office. Brenda had got up to ask Malika a little info on why Traci always sits there in silence and never says a word.

"Malika, I know it's none of my business, but what is wrong with the girl sitting in the corner? She seems to always have a session when I do. She seems like she wants to say something to me, but never does. Is there something wrong with her?" Brenda whispered.

"I don't know Brenda, I stay at my desk and mind my business."

"You mean you've never noticed it before?"

"Brenda... I think... you should sit and wait for Miss Castleberry to come out. She doesn't like me talking about her patients, okay? We don't want to get in trouble, now do we?"

"No I don't want you to lose your job. It's a little scary how she always looks at me. But thanks Malika."

"Sure, Brenda, anytime."

Corrine opened the cherry wood doors of her office suite and called Brenda in. She has always dressed in a nice suit and her glasses always at right in the middle of her face. She was always professional talked to Brenda in a manner that she wished she had gotten from her mother when she was a little girl. It was always so nurturing.

"Hi Brenda. I'm sorry to keep you. Come in and have a seat." Miss Castleberry closed the doors behind her and walked over to her desk. She grabbed her gold pen, notebook started reading past notes.

"It wasn't too long, Miss Castleberry can I call you Corinne?" Brenda said with a devilish smirk on her face as Miss Castleberry turned around and looked back at Brenda in a state of shock.

"Brenda, if you don't mind I like to keep it strictly professional with my patients. Miss C. or Miss Castleberry will do.

My personal life is that, my own personal business. Is that okay with you?" Corrine said in a stern tone.

"I mean, that's fine, but I'm in here to share my own personal business, which I do not enjoy, so I thought I would ask. I'm sorry if I offended you in any way."

"No Brenda, you didn't. I'm sorry. If I expect you to open up to me, I should do the same. So what do you want to talk about? Is there anything you want to ask me?"

Brenda wished she could tell her that she didn't want to talk about anything at all. She knew she had to get these things off her chest before these feelings took over. Brenda had so many questions and feelings but didn't know where to begin.

"Brenda, the floor is yours. Anytime you want to begin."

"Miss Castleberry, I don't know where to begin. I'm mixed up with a bunch of feelings I'm scared." Brenda clutched her purse as if she was afraid of something.

"I understand and I'm here to help you, Brenda. Well, let's start with your mother. How are you and her doing?"

"Well, we had it out before my incident. I asked her for a few dollars for gas to get to my new job. The conversation didn't go as planned." Tears streamed down Brenda's face as she spoke.

"You mean your rape. The conversation between you and your mother took place before your rape."

"You mean my incident, Miss Castleberry. Why do you call it rape?" Brenda began to get angry and her tears dried within seconds.

"Because, Brenda, that's what happened to you. You were raped. How do you feel about that?" Miss C began to write down notes on her notepad noticed Brenda standing up by the door.

"No rape happened to me. I was attacked, yes, but not raped. Why do you want me to remember such horrible things that never happened?"

"Because it did happen, Brenda. You can't pretend that it didn't. The hospital and the police reports clearly show you were raped. We don't have to talk about this now. We can talk about your mother the conversation you had with her. We can address this some other time. I didn't mean to make you angry." Miss C wanted to regain Brenda's trust, so she put down the pen and paper and listened.

"You didn't make me angry, but I wasn't raped. Let's clear that up right now."

"So Brenda, what were you in the hospital for?"

"A man attacked me outside my apartment, but he didn't rape me."

"You don't remember the rape Brenda? Well let's not talk about it. Back to your mother…" Miss Castleberry didn't want to push Brenda any further, she knew what could happen if she did.

"What about her?" Brenda asked while playing with the handles on her purse.

"You said that you and she had a conversation it didn't go well. How did that make you feel?"

"My mother doesn't care about anyone but herself. She could care less about what happened to me about my new job my new position. All she cares about is herself end of story. Is there anything else you want to analyze about my mother?" At this point, Brenda had shut down and didn't want to talk anymore.

"No Brenda, we are here because you wanted my help with your mother and the issues you two were having. I think those issues are deeper than you may realize, Brenda. What happened to you may have triggered some things in you and I think we need to discuss them."

"Miss Castleberry, I think we need to end this right now. You are asking me questions about situations I don't know anything about. You're still trying to get through to my mother. It won't work. She will never accept me as her daughter, a mother, a wife or even a woman for that matter. I think we are done here. I don't want to continue with my session." Brenda grabbed the doorknob and started to walk out when Miss Castleberry pulled her by her arm. Brenda was never one for fighting, but she had to get very forceful with her to make her point.

"Brenda, please, can you wait a minute? Let's start over."

"Get off of me, bitch!" Brenda shoved Corrine so hard that she fell to the floor and her face lit up with fear in her eyes. Corrine recognized that look from her own childhood. She looked at Brenda as if she was afraid of what she would do next. Brenda didn't mean to push Corrine that hard, but she didn't like for anyone to grab her at all. Brenda seemed like another person, the way she came at Corrine.

Corrine approached Brenda with caution. "Brenda, maybe we should sit down and talk about what you're feeling right now, come back and sit down."

"No, leave me alone!" Brenda opened the door and ran out so fast, that she could tell she startled Malika. She jumped back in her chair as if Brenda was about to hurt her.

Brenda looked over in the corner and saw that the girl who had been sitting there was gone. She didn't stop to ask where she went. Brenda wanted to get far away from the office as fast as she could. This was all way too much for her.

Chapter 11
Session Two

"Is she ready for me yet? I had to rush all the way over here from the hospital so I wouldn't miss my appointment."

"Yes, Traci, have a seat and she will be right with you." Malika said in a mildly nervous tone.

"Miss Castleberry, your other client is here to see you."

"Thanks, Malika, give me a few minutes and then you can send her in." Corrine noticed that Malika's facial expression seemed a bit confused and afraid. "Malika, are you okay? I get the feeling you want to ask me something."

"Well, Miss C, doesn't it seem odd to you the way Brenda was acting. She's never done that before. Then Traci shows up when she doesn't even have an appointment today. But doesn't Brenda know what she's doing?" Malika asked.

"No sweetie, she doesn't understand what she is doing," Corrine responded.

"No Miss C, apparently she doesn't." Malika said in a sarcastic tone.

"Well, then there must be a reason why she is here. Give me five minutes and send her in. Oh and Malika, Brenda isn't aware, okay?" Miss C said.

"No problem, Miss C." As Malika walked out of Miss C's office, she noticed Traci staring at her for no reason. She didn't like Miss C's clients looking at her as if she had done something to them, so she would offer them something to drink or to eat, to break the tension.

"Traci, are you hungry? Miss C usually has some snacks and soda in our break room. I can grab some for you if you like?"

"No, thank you. I'm fine."

"Well, if you need anything, be sure to let me know. She will be right out."

"Thanks." Traci said in a childlike tone.

Five minutes passed quickly Corrine still had Traci waiting for her. She started to get real fidgety increasingly impatient.

"How long is she going to take in there? I have some place I need to be."

"I'm sure it won't be long, Traci. Give her a few more moments, okay?" At that moment, Corrine came out of her office very flustered. She immediately walked over to Malika's desk and gave her a note then she approached Traci.

"I'm sorry, Traci, I don't think we have an appointment today, but what can I help you with?" Miss C could tell that something was wrong.

"Miss Castleberry, I need your help before I get into some really big trouble. I didn't have anyone else to turn to."

"Okay come in let's talk about it."

"Thank you for seeing me on such short notice. I really appreciate it. I didn't know where else to turn. I'm afraid I may lose everything because of my damn mother. I can't let this happen, Miss Castleberry I can't." Traci felt that she could express to Corrine what was going on.

"Calm down Traci. Talk to me and tell me what seems to be the problem."

"Well, you know my mother has a problem with drugs and for the last few years, I've been her supplier. I steal morphine from my job and supply her with it. To make matters worse, her so-called husband, my stepfather, has gotten her into some shit. I know it!"

"Well, how do you know he did? Do you have proof of any of this? Also, why would you jeopardize your future and your sister's future for your mother? You know how she is." Corrine pleaded.

"She's my mother what will she do without me? I have to."

"Well then, if you feel you have to for your mother's sake, then why show up in my office? Why come to me with this? You know if there is illegal stuff going on, I will have to report it. I don't think you want that, do you, Traci?"

This was what Traci didn't want to hear, another lecture when all she wanted was help with her mother. "I knew I couldn't trust you. I don't know why I thought I could come to you for anything. I'm going to have to figure this out by myself. Even if it means I have to…" Traci looked at Corrine long and hard before she finished her sentence.

"Before you do what?"

"Nothing, I know what I have to do."

"Do you, Traci? Do you really? Because I don't think you have a clue as to what's really happening to you. But I think I can help you with that."

"You think you know me, Miss C, but you have no idea what I'm going through right now. No idea! Sometimes I wish I could crawl up in a corner and die. I could kill my mother for what she's putting me through." Traci said as she began to cry uncontrollably.

"I understand the frustration you must feel, but that's not the answer, we both know that. So why don't we talk about this a little more…"

On the other side of the office…

"Can I help you with something, sir?" Malika asked the gentlemen who entered the office.

"Yes, I'm here to see that young therapist behind those doors." one of the men said.

"And what might your name be?" Malika asked as if she was interested in more than the name.

"The name is Trey baby. What might your name be, sweet thing? You sure are pretty." He was sizing her up like a piece of meat.

"Unless you have an appointment with the therapist, I'm going to have to ask you to leave." Malika closed the appointment book because she knew from the looks of them they weren't regular clients.

"Oh, I don't have an appointment, but she will see me. Let her know Trey is here. Will you do that for me, baby?"

"Let me see if I can reach her."

VOICES IN THE DARK

"Yes, why don't you do that for me, love? I will be right here waiting."

As Malika went to knock on Corrine's door as she and Traci were walking out. Traci was in complete shock. She couldn't believe that she was face to face with Trey he was at Miss Castleberry's office. *What was Trey doing here how did he know Miss Castleberry?*

"Trey! Are you following me?"

With the toothpick hanging from his lips his eyes gazing over at Corrine, he answered Traci with a slick comment. "I don't have to follow you, Traci. I know where you are at all times. Always remember that."

Traci walked up to Trey and stood eye to eye to him. "I hate you! Do you hear me, Trey? I hate you!" Traci wasn't afraid of Trey. She knew deep down inside he was weak inside.

"Look here, little girl, my business is with your therapist, isn't that right?" Trey cut his eyes over to Corrine and stared at her as if to let her know she better agree to see him or else.

Traci looked back at Corrine questioning why she would meet with him after all Traci had told her about Trey. Did she call him after what she told her was she

EBONI CHASE   112

on Trey's payroll like everyone else? Lots of questions were running through Traci's mind that only Miss Castleberry could answer.

"Is he telling the truth, Miss C? How could you do this to me? How could you?"

Corrine, looking confused, answered "Traci, it's not what you think. I had no idea he would be here, nor did I call him. He has nothing to do with our sessions, I promise you."

"No, Traci. Baby, this has nothing to do with you. So I suggest you leave us alone."

Traci looked back at Corrine with tears of disappointment in her eyes. She didn't know which one to believe. At that moment, she got a call on her cell phone from Miss Drake, the hospital director where she worked.

"Hello…"

"Traci, I specifically remember telling you to see me before you left to go home."

"I know, Miss Drake, but I had to see my therapist on my lunch hour. It's part of my mother's court case that I do so. I'm so sorry about all of this I am on my way back now."

"You better be, I need to discuss something serious with you. I will be waiting for you for another hour." Traci brushed past Trey and Corrine as they headed into her office.

Traci wondered to herself what that meeting was about. Traci glanced over at Malika, who was behind the desk on the phone. She started to think to herself that they were all against her. At this point, Traci trusted no one with her personal business, not even Corrine.

Corrine was alarmed to see Trey in her office, as she had no idea what he wanted with her. She'd never told anyone about her sessions with Traci nor the other girls, so she was not quite sure as to why Trey and his henchmen had showed up at her office.

"So, to what do I owe this pleasure? Trey, right?"

"Yeah, that's right, baby. The name is Trey. See, we seem to have a problem with some of your patients. I think that with some help from you, we can all come to some type of an agreement come up with a quick resolution."

"I don't understand what you mean, Mr. Trey. Oh, what are their names?" Two tall linebacker-looking men were standing right behind Trey as if they were his personal henchmen.

"Oh, don't worry about their names, they're with me."

"Okay, but if you don't mind, Mr. Trey, anyone that enters my office, must speak their name. You're here to do business and this is how I do my business. Is that clearly understood?"

"Oh, I see nothing has changed. You were always a sassy bitch."

"Don't use that tone with me, I'm not the one, trust me. You don't want to do this dance with me. What is it that you want?" Corrine glared back at Trey with a sinister smile to let him know he or his boys didn't intimidate her.

"I don't want anything. It's more like what you're going to do for me." Trey said as he sat down.

"What I'm going to do for you? Little boy, please there is nothing that you or any of those other little boys behind you can make me do, nothing. Oh and I didn't invite you to stay, so don't get comfortable. You're not welcome here."

"You're meeting with four ladies, am I right?" Trey remained seated.

"I don't know what you're talking about. Don't assume that you know anything about my business nor do you know any of my clients, Mr. Trey. I doubt you know anyone outside of Traci, you're stepdaughter. Oh, didn't think I knew that little secret did you?"

"Lady, I don't care what secret you think you know, but there's a lot that you obviously forgot since you left this community. I suggest you dig a little deeper into those ladies that you're counseling start asking yourself some serious questions. Like how did I know you were dealing with four women? Four different women are they so different?" Trey said as Corrine became very afraid.

There was no way of knowing who her clients were what their sessions were about. She took pride in her work for over fifteen years in the business. It made her very uneasy to know that he knew this information she began to question and replay her sessions with the girls in her mind.

"Look, I don't know what you're talking about I am not doing anything for you or your little thug friends over there."

"Well, I will take that as you will think about it this video I got here in my hand with you as the star will all of a sudden appear on every street corner there is. Do you know what I'm talking about now? Miss C Low?"

Corrine couldn't believe what he called her. That was her name years ago when she was high and being pimped out by her sister. But how did he get a hold of that tape? How did he know where to find her? Trey and his goons left the office he blew a kiss at Malika on his way out. Malika rolled her eyes and rushed into the office to see if Miss Castleberry was all right.

"Miss C, what was he doing here? Do you know him?" Malika asked.

Confused and scared Corrine said, "I did a long time ago." She thought to herself, it couldn't be. It can't be. "Malika, please cancel all my afternoon appointments, I have to go home and check on a few things."

"Okay, what shall I tell Shalae?"

"I need to handle some business. So tell Shalae to bring her journal with her when she comes. As a matter of fact, call Brenda too and try to catch Traci as well and schedule them all for a week from today. Make sure they all bring their letters with them."

"I will. But wouldn't Brenda tell Traci? And are you sure you're going to be okay?"

"Yes, make sure you do as I ask. I have a few loose ends to tie up."

Chapter 12
Going crazy…

What is happening to me? I can't quite understand. I want to get home and crawl into my bed never see the outside world. Who was that girl why was she following me everywhere I went? I hadn't noticed her before, but she was at the hospital now Miss Castleberry's office. She never spoke to me. She would sit and stare at me as if she knew me. I needed to clear my head and rest. I can't go back to my apartment for fear the police didn't catch the man that did this to me, so I will go to my mother's house. Regardless of what our relationship is, I can tolerate her to be safe. I'm going to call her and tell her what happened to me directly, Brenda thought to herself.

"Ma, it's me, Brenda…" Before she could say anything else, Brenda's mother cut her off again.

"I know who it is. Before you even begin, how did you allow a man to rape you in front of your own apartment? You're so stupid." Brenda's mother said.

"Ma! How could you say something like that to me? I didn't allow him to do anything to me. He forced his way into my car when I was on my way to work. I tried to fight back, but he was stronger than me he didn't rape me. Why is everyone saying I was raped?" Brenda was shocked by her mother's comments, but not surprised that she said what she said.

"That's because you're weak, Brenda. You were always weak, even when you were a little girl you're even weaker as a grown ass woman. So I see you're going to deny that the rape ever happened? You probably led him on like you did your..." Brenda's mother stopped herself in mid-sentence.

"My what, Ma? Go ahead and say it! Let me hear you at least acknowledge what happened to me as a little girl and a teenager. Let me hear you say it at least once! Please, say it out loud!" Brenda asked in anger as she started to cry.

"Look, Brenda I will not admit to anything that never took place. The only reason why I believed you this time is because the police showed up at my door asking me questions. When they said you were in the hospital, I believed them." Brenda's mother said with such conviction in her voice as if she really hated her own daughter.

"Ma, I don't have anywhere else to go. You are all I have left. The kids are all away and I need to be here for work. Please,

Ma, don't do this to me…please don't."
Brenda couldn't believe what her mother
was saying she fell to her living room floor
and began to cry hysterically.

"Goodbye, Brenda… I can't help
you." Brenda's mother hung up the phone,
leaving Brenda crying alone.

All Brenda could do was call on the
only family she had left, her Auntie Linda
and Cousin Eva. Brenda managed to get
some of her things together and called her
cousin, Eva to bring her to her Aunt Linda's
house. She was hoping to get some rest and
find some solace maybe some much-needed
answers. I can't believe how much of a bitch
my mother is. One day she will pay for that,
one day her world will come crashing down
on her and I will be nowhere in sight to help
her. She said to herself as she dialed her
cousin, Eva.

"Eva, its Brenda. Can you please
come and get me?"

"Brenda where in the hell did you
go? We have been searching the entire
hospital for you. We looked everywhere for
you. You have to go back. You can't
discharge yourself. I will be there in a few
minutes to bring you back. I will be there
every step of the way we will get through
this together. I'm on my way."

Leave the hospital? What the hell was she talking about? I swear everyone around me must be going crazy.

Eva had hung up the phone, leaving Brenda staring at the receiver, wondering what she was talking about. Brenda was so confused. The nurse who came to see her discharged her from the hospital. She remembers signing paperwork to be released. So what was Eva talking about? It wasn't like I got up and walked out, Brenda thought. None of this was making any sense at all.

Since Eva was on her way to pick her up, Brenda grabbed a few clothes and packed a small suitcase and a travel bag. She walked around her brownstone asking herself why was this happening to me now? She was getting herself together then all of a sudden this starts to happen to her... but why now?

As Brenda started to grab her wallet, she wanted to see her face, so she walked into her bathroom to see what he did to her. She opened the medicine cabinet, grabbed the sleeping pills she had then closed the medicine cabinet. She noticed something extremely wrong. What is she doing in my apartment? It can't be! Brenda thought. She turned around and no one was there.

Moments later, her downstairs intercom buzzer rang.

"Who is it?"

"It's me, Brenda, Eva. Let me up." Eva had gotten there quickly, but then Eva worked around the corner from Brenda's apartment. Maybe she was at work when I called her. I never did ask her. Brenda thought to herself.

"Brenda, you really need to move to a place with an elevator. Those stairs are way too much. I mean I like exercise like anyone else, but damn! Are you ready to go back to the hospital?"

"Eva, I never checked my own self out of the hospital. I am not going crazy because there was a nurse that had paperwork and everything for me to sign. Then I drove myself to my therapy appointment. Are you telling me that none of that took place?"

Eva looked at Brenda with a concerned and confused look on her face. That's when she took her by the hand and sat Brenda down in the living room. "Brenda I don't know what you think you did. But the nurses never checked you out of the hospital no paperwork was signed. They came looking for you to give you your painkillers after the detectives left for another case within the hospital you were gone. They looked everywhere for you, but couldn't find you. That's when the detectives showed up at your moms and she had no clue, so they told her what happened."

"Eva, you're starting to scare me. Why would I walk out of the hospital? There was a nurse or maybe she was an assistant nurse, but I'm telling you she signed me out of the hospital! Dammit Eva! Why are you looking at me like you don't believe me? So tell me how the hell did you get here so fast?" Eva stared at Brenda and started to smile as if to dismiss what she had asked her.

Eva grabbed Brenda's things and proceeded to the door. Eva smiled at Brenda rubbed her hair softly like a mother would to her daughter and said, "Let's go Brenda, we will fix this together. I promise you."

"Fix what, Eva? There's nothing wrong with me! Why does everyone act like I'm crazy and making up stories? First Momma treats me like she hates my guts and it's apparent you do too, Eva. Who's next?"

Eva let out a deep breath and demanded Brenda to come back with her to the hospital. "Brenda, come with me I promise in the morning we can discuss everything. But first you really do need to get some rest."

"Discuss what, Eva? Are you keeping secrets from me too? Please don't tell me you are, I can't take much more of this!" Brenda was all up in Eva's face as if she was fed up with everyone around her, including her own cousin, Eva.

"Brenda, I am not keeping anything from you, so don't come at me like I'm the enemy! But you have me a little concerned. You mysteriously walked out of a hospital saying you were discharged and you weren't. I don't even know how you got to your apartment! I don't know what's wrong, but I do know that you need some rest we can think about what to do in the morning. Is that a deal?"

Brenda nodded her head yes and took a long last look around her apartment. She knew she would have to eventually move she wouldn't feel comfortable coming back to the place where the attack happened. Eva and Brenda walked out of the apartment and headed downstairs to Eva's car. Brenda was afraid she would see her attacker, so she put on some shades and a dirty old baseball cap. She quickly ran to the corner where Eva had parked. Brenda took another last look at her brownstone.

"Brenda…Brenda…Brenda???"

"What?"

"Get in the car and let's go. Don't look back if it hurts too much to do so, okay?"

Brenda got in the car and shut the door. Her cell phone rang and it was Malika from Miss Castleberry's office.

"Hi Malika, yes, I can do that. But why?"

As Eva drove away, Brenda pondered to herself… am I really going crazy?

VOICES IN THE DARK

Chapter 13
Trouble…

I can't believe Miss Castleberry betrayed me like that. I wanted to stay behind to find out what Trey had to discuss with Miss Castleberry, but I also needed to get back to work to find out what Miss Drake wanted. *I didn't know if my stealing from the job was about to be exposed if I was going to get the promotion I applied for at the hospital. Either way I knew what I needed to do, but I was afraid to stop.* Traci's thoughts were running rampant, yet quietly in her mind. Traci arrived at the hospital to her surprise Carmen was still at their station. She was supposed to be home already.

"Carmen, why are you still here?" Traci asked as she took off her jacket and put her name badge on to make it appear that she had been there for a little while. Traci was about twenty-five minutes late from when Miss Drake told her to be back.

"Girl, I was trying to cover for you! Miss Drake seems pissed off! I don't know who got her panties in a bunch, but she told me to stick around. She has all of us staying late, something about a floor meeting with the staff." Carmen whispered.

Traci couldn't help but think to herself that Miss Drake must've found out about her stealing. Those floor meetings were regularly scheduled on a monthly basis they had one last week. As Carmen and Traci were talking, she noticed Miss Drake coming down the hall and didn't look pleased at all. She was coming right in their direction with a look that could kill.

"Nice of you to finally grace us with your presence, Traci. Carmen, don't you have something to do before the meeting begins?"

Carmen quickly grabbed her things to finish her rounds. "Yes, Miss Drake, I do." As Carmen rushed off, she quietly with her eyes wished Traci luck.

Traci turned to Miss Drake. "Miss Drake, I'm so sorry about being late, but I can explain everything. You see…"

"Save it, Traci! I don't want to hear your excuses about why you were late. What I want to know is why? Why would you want to ruin a career you have yet to begin so early?" Traci didn't know what she was talking about she damn sure wasn't about to tell on herself, so Traci decided to play along with Miss Drake to see exactly what she was talking about.

"Miss Drake, I really can explain everything. I can, if you let me."

"Traci, how can you explain to me your mother lurking around the hospital looking for drugs saying you told her where they were?"

What the hell did she say to me? My mother lurking for drugs! Traci thought. "Miss Drake, I have no idea what you are talking about! I would never tell my mother anything like that! It goes against her court case and I could lose custody of my baby sister!"

"Traci, do you expect me to believe you with the way you've been acting? I want you to know the board won't hear about this little incident from me, but I can't cover you the next time she pulls a stunt like this. I sent her back home in a cab," Miss Drake said.

"I assure you Miss Drake, it will never happen again." Traci promised, knowing she couldn't keep it.

"Well, I hope not, for your sake. I think you should go home and see how she is doing. You're okay to miss this one meeting. I believe you have more important business to attend to."

"Yes ma'am, I do. Thank you for speaking with me privately Miss Drake. I appreciate that."

"Continue to do your job and do not cause any more problems, Traci or I will see to it that you never work in another hospital. Do we understand each other?" Miss Drake grabbed her things and started to head back down the hall to the meeting.

"Yes, we do."

"Goodnight, Traci"

"Goodnight, Miss Drake."

All Traci could think to herself was killing that bitch! She couldn't believe her mother would do this to her. She never told her where anything was. Traci grabbed her things and punched out. She was going to have a nice long talk with her mother. What she really wanted to do was to kill her mother with her bare hands for almost making her lose her damn job behind her bullshit. Traci decided to try to calm down and call her first. She was pissed off!

"Ma! How could you fucking do this to me? Did you hear what I said, Ma? How could you do this to me?" Traci couldn't understand her mother because she was crying like a hysterical woman. She couldn't half make out what her mother was saying to her.

"Ma, calm down! What man? What are you talking about? He did what? I will be right there…"

Traci ran out the hospital with Miss Drake, the job, Trey, her sister and Miss Castleberry all on her mind. Her mind was racing and she was enraged! Traci jumped in her car and headed to her mother's house to find out what was going on. Her cell started to ring with a call from Miss Castleberry's office.

"What do you want?" Since she knew her office number, she thought it was Miss C calling, but it was Malika.

"Sorry Malika, I thought you were your boss. Yes, I guess I can do that, but why?" Malika didn't disclose any information as to why she was calling, only instructions. If it were not for Traci's mother's case, she wouldn't have agreed.

Chapter 14
Confusion

Shalae arrived at the hospital looking for her mother but she was nowhere to be found. She wasn't expecting to run into Miss C in the hospital. Shalae looked everywhere for her mother and couldn't find her. She checked all the stations and that's when she decided to go ask someone where she was.

"Hi, my name is Shalae, I received a call earlier today that my mother was brought here to the hospital. I received it at the same time I received the call about my fiancé." The nurse didn't respond to any of her questions. She turned away from Shalae as if she wasn't standing there.

"Excuse me, miss…did you hear what I said?" The nurse turned around with such a nasty disposition that it made Shalae feel like she really didn't want to deal with her at all. The nurse was busy writing and didn't appear as if she had anything else to do.

"I don't know who or what you are talking about. What is your mother's name?"

"Look, I had a really long day, as I'm sure you have. There is no need to be nasty or short with me! My mother's name is Mary… Mary Johnson. Is she here or was she released? Can somebody tell me what happened?"

"Sweetie, are you sure that's your mother's name?"

"Yes! I think I would know my own mother's name."

The nurse walked away from Shalae with a confused look on her face. She put her clipboard down, walked over to Shalae and grabbed her by the arm. "Miss I think you should come with me. I'm sure that there is a good explanation for all of this the doctor can straighten this out."

"Let go of my arm!" Shalae demanded and pulled away from the nurse. The other nurses stopped what they were doing and completely had their eyes on Shalae and the nurse as if Shalae was crazy.

"Miss there is no need to be hostile when all I am trying to do is help you." The nurse still had a tight grip on her arm and she would not let it go.

"Help me? You are looking at me like I'm crazy. I know what my mother's name is, she gave birth to me! I got a call earlier around the same time I got a call about my fiancé, Brian. I was told that she was here beaten up badly. I know who did it, but I need to see her. So if you could please tell me what room she is in right now!"

The nurse hesitated, but she did as Shalae asked and went back behind the nurse's station to look at her charts. She acted as though the name didn't exist, as if Shalae was making it up. Shalae could tell she wasn't really looking she kept eyeing her and the nurses around her.

She walked over to Shalae with a concerned look on her face and said, "Miss if you could wait right here for a minute. I need to check my other chart. It will take a few seconds."

At this point, Shalae was getting tired of the runaround and decided to walk the halls of the hospital herself. The nurses especially this one, was getting on her last nerve. "Look, lady! I really need you to find my mother unless you want me to start screaming her name up and down these halls, I suggest you either get your ass from around that fucking desk and help me find her or I am about to become your worst headache!" Shalae said as she flipped the clipboard across the nurses' station.

Feeling the wrath of Shalae's frustration, the nurses began to help her look for her mother. The other nurses behind the desk looked very afraid but more confused than anything. Shalae could tell that they were all hiding something. What was it?

The nurse took Shalae to another nurses' station to check more charts. They must've looked at about ten different charts her mother's name was nowhere to be found. Shalae started to wonder if this was some sick joke that Brian was playing on her as payback for what she did to him, but she definitely was sure about what the police had told her. They said that the hands of her father had brought her mother to the hospital as well.

Hours passed with no sign of Shalae's mother anywhere. "Miss, I'm sorry we couldn't find who you were looking for. I wish I could be of more help, but I have checked all of my stations I worked and covered for people throughout today and last night. We have no Jackie registered here or even coming through the ER within the last forty-eight hours. I'm so sorry."

"Thanks… I wish I knew what was going on. But thank you the same."

As Shalae walked away from the nurse she wondered to herself why the police would tell her that her mother was brought into the ER covered in bruises as if someone had beaten her? It couldn't be Brian; he couldn't talk because of the glass.

Shalae made sure of that. Maybe the police had the wrong person, but they said her mother's name.

Shalae must have wandered around the hospital for hours before she actually went back to Brian's room to see how he was doing. All Shalae kept thinking was *what was she going to do now?* She had a baby on the way she was going to be a single parent. How was she going to raise this child alone, knowing that the father abuses her? How can she get out of this dilemma that she had gotten herself into?

Shalae made her way back to Brian's room and to her surprise he was sound asleep. She pulled up one of the chairs and sat down so she could think. She had to find a way to get Brian out of her life. He was no good for her, but the worst part was that he wasn't good to her either. She had literally fallen down the same path as her parents, an abusive relationship with an innocent baby about to be born. She didn't want this for her life or for any child that she would have. But now that fear was indeed a reality and she had to find a way to get through it.

Brian was sleeping so peacefully, but she knew that once he woke up and saw her, there would be hell to pay. He was not going to let Shalae live this down. He would make her pay for this every day if he could. Shalae had to teach him that he couldn't continue beating her. It had to stop. She is the only one that can stop it. Unfortunately, it took her to get violent in order for him to get a hint, but it was going to be either him or her.

Two hours later…

"Miss… Miss… visiting hours are over, are you his wife? If so, then I apologize." Shalae had fallen asleep in the chair and was awakened by a tap on her shoulder. "What time is it? How long have I've been asleep?"

"It's almost ten o'clock. You must've been here for a long time. I'm sorry to wake you, but you were sleeping so peacefully. Your husband is in good hands." The nurse said smiling.

"No, we are not married yet. He is my fiancé. I didn't realize I was asleep for that long. Is he going to be alright?" Shalae sat upright in the chair to stretch her legs.

"Yes, he is, thank God. We called you in time. At first, we didn't think he was going to make it, but from the looks of the wound, the doctor did a good job. He may not be able to talk, but he will live."

"Wait a minute! Did you call me earlier about Brian?" Shalae stood up from the chair beside Brian's bed in complete shock.

"I did. You sounded like you didn't even care, but I believe in people I knew you would come." The nurse said as she checked Brian's IV.

"Then you're the same nurse that called about my mother. The police came to my job at the same time I got the call. They said the nurse that called them about my mother was the same nurse that called me. Do you know where my mother is?" Shalae asked.

"Yes, I did call you, but didn't they tell you? I left word at the nurse's station to tell you." The nurse said as she held Shalae's hand and touched her shoulder.

"Tell me what? All I know is that I walked all over this hospital to look for my mother with another not so nice nurse. She told me that none of the charts stated that she was even here. I gave up and came to Brian's room to sit and think. The next thing I knew, you were waking me up. So please, do you know where my mother is? I am really worried about her." Shalae said as she started to cry.

"Sweetie, your mother was bandaged up and discharged. She became very nervous she stated that the person who beat her up was in the hospital," the nurse said.

"You mean my dad? He's been abusing her for years. I knew it was him and he must've followed her here in the ambulance."

"No baby, I think you are mistaken. Maybe I do have the wrong person. Your mother was not on this floor. She came into the ward with broken bones and bruises. She said a man attacked her she was running away from him. She stated that he was inside the hospital. When I asked her if she had any family, she named you as her relative. I treated her then she left without signing any release papers. Miss, are you okay? You don't look so well... maybe you should have a seat." The nurse tried to get Shalae to take a seat. Shalae felt numb all over. She couldn't believe what this nurse was saying to her. Where was her mother? What man beat her up other than her father? What the hell was going on?

Shalae's cell went off as she quietly she prayed to God that it was her mother. "Shalae, this is Malika, Miss C asked me to call you."

"Malika, this is not a good time. I have so much going on right now that I can't begin to explain. I will be at my next appointment, in fact, I may need to schedule it earlier," Shalae said as she wiped the tears from her eyes.

"Shalae, she wants you to be here Friday for a meeting with some other women." Malika said.

"For what? Especially in a group with other women, I am not ready for that."

"Shalae, this needs to be done, so please be on time. See you then."

As quick as Malika called her, she hung up the phone. Now Shalae had the task of finding out what the hell happened to her mother.

God, where is my mother? Shalae thought. I need you now more than ever.

Chapter 15
Reunions pt. 2…

Corrine couldn't believe this bastard had the nerve to show up in her office. "Lord, please forgive my language! Please make me understand why this is happening to me now. I made sure I did everything you guided me to do, so this wouldn't happen. Only you, God, know the will of what is to come. I ask you please, spare the children." Corrine prayed as she drove to her old stomping ground where she used to live. She arrived at the same run down projects she grew up in. Corrine was elated the day she packed up and left this place over twenty-five years ago. She vowed she would never return, except to help the children of the community and fix her own sins. As she parked the car and started to get out, she thought to herself, *she promised me that she wouldn't open her mouth about our little pact. But somehow, she must've told someone. It wasn't by coincidence that Trey showed up at my office with a tape.*

The neighborhood was still the same; filled with a bunch of drunks, crack heads and a sprinkle of prostitutes. She counsels the children and some of the children's children of most of the people within this community in her office. None of them knows whether they will make it day by day. She had made a promise to herself back then in fact they both promised that the girls would stay out of this bullshit. Somehow, someone had forgotten that promise…

Corrine banged on the door so loud that other neighbors opened their doors to be nosey. There was always something going on in the neighborhood so it was normal for the loud noise and screaming to be heard in the hallway.

"Open up the door, bitch! You have some serious explaining to do! We are going to get this straight once and for all!"

"I'm coming… stop banging on my damn door!" When she saw Corrine's face, she laughed and turned around. She continued laughing as she went back into her apartment, leaving the door open.

"Who the hell are you calling a bitch? Why the hell were you knocking on my damn door like you the police or something! You know people around here get killed for that! What the fuck do you want? You know Traci is on her way over here, so don't make this visit longer than five fucking minutes… now speak." Jackie said as she went to sit down in her dusty old red chair in her living room.

"This is going to take longer than five minutes, Jackie! How could you do this to me? Why would you send him to my office? Wait a minute… what happened to your face?" Corrine asked as if she was really concerned about Jackie's welfare.

"None of your damn business and don't come in here like you're going to save me now. I've been waiting years for that… and I'm still waiting! First of all, I haven't done anything to you except keep your dirty secrets all these years. Don't come into my house acting all high and mighty bitch! I think you forgot where you at! Secondly, send who to your office?" Jackie said with a nasty tone as she blew smoke from her cigarette in Corrine's face.

"Trey, that's who! You sent him to my office with that tape! How did he get it, Jackie? Only you and I know about that tape!"

"Is that all you're worried about? I thought it was something more serious." Jackie chuckled as she lit her cigarette and leaned back in her dirty recliner."

"Jackie, will you stop fucking around! It's very serious! You are messing with my career!"

"Bitch, your career? Don't you mean my career?" Jackie yelled at the top of her lungs.

"Can we talk about this woman to woman? No one needed to get a hold of that tape. We are not talking about your life, but for the sake of the girl's lives too. Jackie, you have to get that tape back from Trey. I can't tell you how to do it, but you have to." Corrine sat down and tried to plead with Jackie, but it wasn't working.

"Now you want to talk woman to woman? Don't you mean sister to sister? I don't have to do nothing but get high or die! How dare you come into my motherfucking house after all these damn years and demand I cover your high-class ass! I've been covering for you and your secrets for more than twenty years. Why now? Because, you may lose your precious practice or is it that daughter of yours you are worried about?"

"What did you say?" Corrine didn't think she heard her right.

"You heard me... your daughter. Oh, you didn't think I knew about her, did you? There is plenty about you that I know. Don't try me bitch. You are walking on thin ice around here. We all have been keeping track of you throughout the years."

"Jackie, you have no idea what you are talking about! Leave Malika out of this!"

"Well, Miss high class, you tell me how can I leave your daughter out of this? I mean, let's face it. After all her mother damaged goods. Isn't she? Or does Malika know your sorted past Sis?" Jackie said as she let out a light chuckle under her breath.

"Jackie, I am a Christian woman now, but before God here today so help me, if you mention my daughter one more time, I will forget all that Christianity and whoop your ass! Now I want that damn tape back! Find a way to make it happen. Our daughters, yours as well as mine will get a peek into my past journals and really see you for the mother you truly are! Am I making myself clear?" Corrine stood up in Jackie's face to make her statement firm.

"When were you going to finally come see me? When? When were the rest of us going to find out you were back in town? But I guess after what we did to you, you dis-owned your own family huh? After all we did for you...you know what, your five minutes is up miss high class! Get the hell out of my house. I need my beauty rest. I don't think you want Traci to see you here, now do you? After all, we don't know each other, do we? Close the door on your way out." Jackie waved Corrine off to let her know she was no longer paying attention.

"Jackie, after all you did for me? Bitch you got me in the mess I'm in now. That we all are in now! I'm warning you..."

"I'm shaking in my boots, bitch! Oh, I'm not worried about none of my daughters finding the truth about me because they know their mother. I can't say the same for you, can I? Get out!" Jackie slammed the door in Corrine's face as if she was a stranger on private property.

Corrine headed downstairs engulfed with anger. *I hate her with a passion! Somehow I have to get that tape from Trey, but he won't give it to me willingly I know Jackie will not even try to get it. She only cares about herself. She doesn't care about them, like me. She never did. But what could I have done differently back then? I was strung out on drugs and I needed to find my way out. I promised my aunt that I would come back and get them, but I never did... instead, I left them in the hands of two devils and a child molester. Lord, I worked so hard to be able to make amends with all my daughters, but they will never forgive me for what I've done... never.*

"Miss C, what are you doing here?"

A startled Corrine replied, "Traci... I..." She was startled to have bumped into Traci.

"Did you hear about what my mother did at the hospital? I also heard she was attacked. Is that why you're here?"

"Traci, you know your mother, she is fine. How are you? I was wondering about you after you saw your stepfather at my office. I promise you, sweetie, I had no idea he would come to my office." Corrine said as she tried to change the subject.

"I'm sure you didn't, Miss C. When I had a chance to really think about it, I realized by the look in your eyes. I could tell you were as shocked as I was. Is my mother really okay? How bad is her face?" Traci asked.

"She seemed to be okay. Some bruises under her eyes. Do you know who did this to her?"

"I don't know. But I plan to get to the bottom of it, I promise you."

"I wouldn't worry so much about her, Traci. You know she can take care of herself. It was probably one of her tricks."

Traci looked at Corrine as if she saw a ghost. Corrine couldn't tell if it was an expression of hate or confusion. "Miss C, how do you know my mother is still tricking? Did someone tell you that?" Traci asked.

"No, I must've heard it from somewhere." Miss C didn't want to lie to her, but what could she say?

"Miss C, my mother is a good woman deep down inside. She had some hard times. I'm sure you understand that. Didn't you ever go through some hard times?"

"Traci, you have no idea. But go see your mother. I was here visiting another client of mine said hi to your mom. I think I should be going. Oh, Traci, did Malika call you?"

"Yes, as a matter of fact, she did. I never told my mother about our sessions. Have you?"

"No, Traci, those are protected under the HIPAA privacy act. I promise you that know but you and I. You will get the opportunity at some point to address your mother with your thoughts I hope that it will somehow set you free."

"Set me free?"

"You'll understand very soon, Traci. Well, let me go, I will see you on Friday."

"Okay, Miss C, see you Friday."
As Corrine walked down the staircase, she turned back around to see Traci hugging her

mother as she opened the door. All she kept thinking to herself was... *Lord, help us all.*

Chapter 16
Sisters...

"Momma, why didn't you tell me you was attacked? Who did this to your face? Is this why you called me in a panic? I need to know, Momma." Traci asked as she held her mother's chin, examining her bruises.

"Traci, what was I supposed to do? I was worried at first, but I did what I had to. Your momma can handle herself," she said as she took another pull from her Newport.

"That's what I'm afraid of, Momma. I also need to ask you something please don't get mad." Traci said as she sat down on the arm of the chair next to her mother.

"Now Traci, you know how I hate to be questioned. What is it?"

"Were you at the hospital today stealing drugs?"

"I did go to the hospital, but I was looking for you."

"Why, Momma, when you knew I was in therapy with Miss C."

"You need to stay away from that woman. Something is not quite right with her." Traci's mother demanded.

"Momma, there's nothing wrong with her. In fact, she is trying to help me deal with you and our past issues. Momma, did you take anything?"

"Now why would I have to be at the hospital stealing drugs when you provide them for me? I know I'm fucked up, but that would be stupid."

"Momma, about that… I can't do that anymore if I want to keep my job. Miss Drake is on to me, I know it."

"Well Traci, I taught you how to handle those types of people. So do what momma taught you."

"Momma… I'm tired and want something better for myself. By the way, is Nique in her room?"

"Yes, she's fast asleep."

"Well, I want to peek in on her, that's all."

"Go ahead, be my guest," said her mother as she lit another Newport.

When she was a little girl, Traci couldn't wait to get out of this place, so she could only imagine how her baby sister felt. As Traci walked toward her sister's room, she saw that her mother still put her cigarettes out in her drinks never cleans it up. Instead, she leaves it for Traci to do when she comes around.

"Momma, you really need to stop drinking. This place is a mess."

"You don't need to tell me what I shouldn't be doing. You need to do as I say." her mother shouted from the living room.

Traci turned the corner to what used to be her room but was now her little sister's room. She had come by a few weeks back and painted it purple. Purple was Nique's favorite color. Traci wanted to brighten up the place, so Nique wouldn't feel so bad about where she lived. She peeked in on her sister like her mother said to find her sleeping soundly. Traci noticed her bears had fallen off the shelf, so she quietly tiptoed around her room to pick them up. When she picked up the last bear, she noticed a foul smell coming from under the bed.

Traci bent down to see what it was. The lower she got, the stronger it got, but she didn't see anything under the bed. She didn't want to wake her sister, so she started to look for things around the room. When Traci was growing up, it was always a dead mouse somewhere, but that wasn't what she smelled.

When she got up from the floor, she noticed Nique wasn't asleep anymore she was staring right at her with tears in her eyes.

Traci whispered softly to her sister, "Nique go back to sleep. You know how mad Momma gets if you're not sleep. I wanted to check on you, baby. Are you okay?"

Nique looked back at Traci with her pretty brown eyes kept staring at her as the tears continuously streamed down her face.

"What's wrong, baby?" Traci asked as she sat down next to her on the bed. Nique pulled herself up with tears in her eyes and started to roll back the covers. Traci couldn't believe what she saw.

"Momma!" Traci screamed for her mother.

She couldn't contain herself. Traci quickly scooped up her sister; put her in her arms, brushed past her mother carried her right out of that room and headed for the front door.

"Traci, where the fuck are you going with Nique!" Jackie had stood up and walked towards the front door.

"Back the fuck up off of me before I kill you! What did you do to her? How could you let this happen?"

"What did you say to me?" Traci's mother looked like she was about to hit her because of the way Traci had spoken to her.

Traci was ready for her this time, but she didn't do it.

"Momma, I swear on everything I love, you better move the fuck out the way before I kill you with my bare hands. What the fuck did you do to her? Your own fucking daughter! How could you? Move out my way right now!"

When her mother wouldn't move, Traci shoved her out her way, opened the door ran down the stairs. She was praying all the way downstairs. She could hear her mother yelling for her to come back from the top of the stairs. Traci placed Nique in the back seat and headed for the hospital.

"Hold on, Nique, I got you! Baby open your eyes... please... don't... Nique... Nique... Lord, help me please!"

Chapter 17
Confrontations

Brenda really didn't want to be there right now, but she needed to confront her mother on some issues so she can try to understand what is happening to her. Brenda knew her mother would not willingly cooperate with her or anyone, but she had to try. She knew all the answers it was time she answered Brenda's questions truthfully.

"Brenda, are you alright?"

"Yes, Eva, I guess so. But why did you bring me back to the hospital? I don't need to be here."

Eva stared at Brenda as if she felt sorry for her. Eva had given Brenda one of those looks that you give a child who can't stop crying when they are hurt so bad. The only thing that will comfort them is their mother's love. The kind of soothing look Brenda longed for from her own mother.

"Sweetie, you need to be here for a little while longer."

"Eva, please don't try to analyze me! I'm fine. I thought we were going to Aunt Linda's house?"

"Aunt Linda is coming here so don't worry. We want what's best for you, Brenda. Can you please trust us?"

"Trust yawl?"

"Yes, trust us. We only have your best interest at heart."

"Well let's see, the last time I trusted our family, I was molested when I was a little girl. But everyone seems to have fucking amnesia about what happened to me, even my own mother. So why should I trust any of you now?" A feeling of anger came over Brenda like she has never felt before she felt like she could kill Eva for trying to belittle her.

"Brenda, don't you trust me?"

With a confused look on her face, Brenda said aloud, "Brenda? Why are you calling me Brenda?"

"Because that's your name, sweetie. What's wrong with you? Stop acting silly cousin, this is not the time to be playing."

"Who's playing? My name is not Brenda. Sweetie, I think you need to get it right. Why am I in this hospital anyway? Where are we going?"

"Brenda, now this isn't funny. I need you to be serious for a minute. Your mother and my mother are on their way here to meet us."

VOICES IN THE DARK

"Look, I have no clue who you are or what you are talking about, my mother is dead."

"Brenda! That's not funny! Take that back right now! Now I know Auntie Mae doesn't get the mother of the year award, but she is still your mother! So cut it out God doesn't like ugly."

"Eva, why the hell are you yelling at me? Take what back? What are you talking about?"

"Brenda, did you not hear what you said?"

"No, what did I say? Why are you looking at me like I'm crazy?"

"I'm starting to think you are. You really don't remember what you said about your mother?"

"No, I don't. Why are we talking about her anyway when she didn't even see me in the hospital? I don't think that woman has a loving bone in her body anymore."

"She does, Brenda, but we have all been through a lot. So try to be easy on her."

"Easy on her? Eva, you can't be serious! After all she's done to me... even to you. But you don't remember because you never talk about it."

"That's not the first time you have said that to me, Brenda. I wish you would tell me why you are so mad at Auntie Mae. What the hell did she do?"

"I don't want to talk about it where am I supposed to be at anyway? Why did I have to come back to the hospital? I wanted to go to your mom's house. That's the only place I feel safe."

"I brought you back here because it was too soon for you to check out of the hospital. Your face isn't even healed yet from the rape. You need at least a few days to rest."

"I called my damn therapist, so I'm fine. I needed to talk to her something I feel deep down inside is going on with me and I'm not sure what it is."

"Brenda, I wish I could help you. I am trying to hold it all together I have my own issues as well."

"Eva… I was thinking to myself the same thing. Momma did tell me. How? When did you find out?"

"I found out a few weeks ago. Doesn't really matter how… I have it. Now I am in the fight of my life and all I know is that I have to live. I have to."

"I am so sorry to hear this, Eva. You don't deserve this. What did your husband say to you?"

"He left me, Brenda… but I don't want to talk about this right now, we are here to make sure you get better. The nurse is going to come and bring you back to your room for a night. I will be here in the morning to take you to my house then to your therapy session. Remember I am always here for you."

A nurse headed towards Brenda with a wheelchair holding a small cup with two pills. Brenda already knew that this would put her to sleep whether she wanted to go willingly or not. Her cousin Eva kissed her cheek and walked away in the other direction. As Brenda was wheeled away with the nurse, she could only imagine what her cousin was dealing with. Words could not express the emotions that filled her head. She wanted to hug her and cry with her like they did when they were little girls and Brenda's father would do to the both of —that's when it hit her! Brenda turned around, jumped out the wheel chair and ran down the hall toward the front entrance, but Eva was already gone. The nurse came running after her.

"Ma'am, you can't do that! Now get back in this chair. Your family will be here in the morning to get you. What is wrong with you?"

"I'm sorry, something I realized. I will deal with it in the morning, I guess. I'm sorry I didn't mean to make you chase me. I'm normally not like this."

"It's okay. Before I wheel you off, take these meds. Here is some water to wash them down. Then by the time we get to your room, you will be more relaxed. I also have some news that might brighten your mood. I got paged that your mother is waiting in your room for you. Now I bet that makes you feel a lot better."

"My mother? Are you sure you mean my mother? Miss, I think you are talking about the wrong person. My mother wouldn't show her face here."

"Well that's what I was told, so let's see her, shall we."

"I guess I have no choice, now do I?"

The nurse hit the button on the elevator and pushed level two. They got in the elevator and Brenda held her head down because she didn't know what to say to her mother. She didn't believe me when I told her I was raped, so why on earth is she here in the hospital now? Maybe she really did feel something for me. But why did it take me to get raped for her to come around.

Brenda lifted her head and noticed that the same girl from Miss Castleberry's office was in the elevator with her and the nurse. This is the third time they encountering one another. This time, they locked eyes but said nothing. She was covered in so much blood. Brenda wanted so badly to ask what happened to her, but she looked so angry. They both reached level two she ran out the elevator as if someone was chasing her.

"Nurse, what happened to that girl?"

"What girl?" the nurse asked.

"The girl that was in the elevator with us, didn't you see her?"

"Baby, I think those pills are kicking in. We were the only ones in the elevator…"

It can't be! We were the only ones in the elevator. But that girl was the same one I saw at the office, in my house now in the hospital! *God please, what is wrong with me? Am I really going crazy?* Brenda thought.

Brenda and the nurse arrived at her room and sure enough, her mother was standing there in all her glory. Brenda couldn't believe she actually showed up.

Regardless of the reason, she was happy she was there to support her.

"Well here you are, how are you? I'm Nurse Nichols. It's nice to meet you."

Brenda's mother let Nurse Nichols hand remain extended. Her mother never was very sociable.

Nurse Nichols took her hand back and leaned over to Brenda. "Brenda, I will be right outside. You ring this buzzer if you need me, okay sweetie?"

"Thank you, Nurse Nichols, I will." Brenda was holding Nurse Nichols' hand so tightly as if her life depended on it. She was so afraid to let it go. Brenda could tell by the look in Nurse Nichols eyes that she didn't understand what was going on, so Brenda let her hand go. Brenda watched her walk out the room for some reason her fear came back like she was a little girl all over again.

"Momma, will you help me out my chair please? I'm still a little sore."

"Girl you're not cripple some random man fucked you that's all so get over yourself."

"Yes, the nurse was right! My mother was waiting for me in my room. Do you have any compassion at all for me? Or do you hate me that damn much? Why did you even come here?" Brenda was so disgusted by her comment that she wanted her to leave.

"I want you to stop going to see that psychiatrist. I think she had you set up to be raped to set you back."

"Momma! How could you say such a stupid thing like that? She has done nothing but help me, which is more than I can say for you."

"Brenda, listen...there are things."

"Oh, now you want to talk to me, Momma?"

"Forget it! You can find out on your own. He should've killed you while he was raping you!" As her mother finished her sentence, Nurse Nichols walked in and heard what Brenda's mother said to her.

"Ma'am, I'm afraid I'm going to have to ask you to leave this room. You are clearly upsetting my patient that I will not allow while she is under my care."

Brenda's mother brushed past Nurse Nichols. "Under your care? Bitch I tried to care for her for years and she is the devil. So I wish you luck!"

Her mother stormed out the room leaving Nurse Nichols with a shocked look on her face. Brenda didn't even know where to begin to explain to her that...that's how she is. Her mother doesn't love anyone, not even Brenda.

Chapter 18
Baby Sister...

"Nurse! Nurse! Where the fuck is everybody? Someone, anyone please help me! Nique, baby hold on, I'm getting help for you baby. Please hold on." Traci screamed throughout the emergency room.

"Ma'am, please hold down the noise. We have patients that are sleeping. Now tell me what's wrong?"

"Fuck your patients! My baby sister is bleeding and bruised! Please help her now!"

"Okay...Okay...where is she?"

Traci headed over to Nique's frail body, which she had put down in one of the waiting room chairs, but she had slipped into unconsciousness. The nurse grabbed her and about three other nurses ran with them down the hall into an empty room. One of the nurses held Traci back as the other nurse shut the door.

"Nique! Nique!" Traci screamed for her, but she couldn't hear her. Traci kept trying to fight the nurse to let her in to be with her sister, but they wouldn't let her in.

"Sweetie, we need to get some information from you about her while they work on her, now come with me."

"But I promised her, don't you understand? I promised. Big sisters always keep their promises. How could I let this happen to her! I promised. Nique! Nique!" Traci was overcome with grief and could barely stand up straight.

"Your sister is in the best of care, I promise. Come with me so I can get all the information we need, in order to treat her. Do you happen to know her blood type? We need this information in case she needs a transfusion."

"Blood? Oh my God. Momma, what did you do?" Traci screamed.

"Are you saying that your mother did this to her?" the nurse asked, but Traci couldn't control herself. She was overcome with emotions to the point that she collapsed on the floor and blacked out.

Chapter 19
Corrine's home

The one place where Corrine could gather her thoughts was in her home. Back at her brownstone located in the heart of the city but far enough from the community that held all her deep darkest secrets Corrine began to ponder her situation. She needed to get to the bottom of why Malika is acting this way. This wasn't like her. She has been disrespectful and downright ignorant for the last few weeks. *Lord, I hope this girl isn't pregnant. That's all I need right now in the midst of all of this other drama I have going on is to become a grandmother. But then, Malika has always been a good quiet girl, so I don't understand where all of this is coming from...* As so many thoughts ran through Corrine's mind, she started making the necessary calls for her patients. She needed to understand why these things were taking place. Corrine went upstairs to knock on Malika's door where she had the music blasting as if she was in a mansion somewhere. The walls in the brownstone weren't that thick and Corrine knew in about five minutes, Miss Thorpe, who was in the connecting brownstone would start banging on her door about the noise. She didn't need that drama tonight.

"Malika, open up this door. Malika? Malika I said open the door?" Corrine screamed her name three times until the music was finally turned down but Malika still didn't open the door.

Corrine heard some movement and stumbling around. "Malika? Is everything okay in there? Open up this door." Malika finally opened the door and the room was filled with smoke. The smell of weed engulfed her room.

"Yes, mother, what is it?" Malika said as she opened the door and went back to what she was doing.

"Girl, don't you question me like I am some type of guest! What the hell do you think you're doing?"

"I was relaxing." Malika answered with arrogance in her voice.

"Oh, so you're relaxing? Not in my house you're not! Have you lost your mind? Smoking weed as if you paying bills up in here. Are you crazy? You must want me to catch a charge."

"Oh we wouldn't want you to lose your precious practice and or your precious patients."

"What makes you think I would lose my practice? What has gotten into you lately, Malika? Haven't I provided for you? Fed you? Made sure you had all the nice things in life along with a nice place to live? Why are you starting to act so ungrateful?" Corrine asked.

"Ungrateful? I didn't ask for any of these things!"

"I know, Malika, but a mother always wants the absolute best for her child. You didn't have to ask, I want you to have nice things. Why can't we get along? I know I am barely here, but there are a whole lot of things that you don't and wouldn't understand."

"Try me, Mother. You are never around and you never talk to me. I'm going to be eighteen soon and you still treat me like I am a child."

"That's because you still do childish things. You are my child who still lives under my roof. Until you get a place of your own, pay your own bills, drive your own car that I don't pay for… then you get to ask questions about my practice. You have two more years before you are eighteen my darling daughter. Until then I need your help and cooperation on some things. This is why I made you my assistant. So we can be closer see each other every day. Isn't that what you wanted?"

"Yeah, I guess…"

"So what's with the weed? Why are you smoking all of a sudden? You hate when I smoke cigarettes."

"Ma, I've been smoking since I was thirteen. Shows you how much you really pay attention to me."

"Excuse me, Miss?" Corrine looked at her child in a different light what she hadn't noticed, was that she was right. Malika had grown up when she wasn't looking.

"Yes Mother, since thirteen. But I swear I never did it in the house, but I would have a cigarette before I got home from school."

"Well, I can't say much to you now, you're almost eighteen. So I tell you what. Ditch the weed I won't bother you so much about the cigarettes, deal?"

"When did you become so cool?"

"Oh baby girl, I was always cool. Cooler than you think! I want us to be closer that's all, okay Malika?"

"That's all I want, Momma, but you're never around your clients all come before me. They always did. Personally, I'm sick of dealing with it."

"Now see Malika, we were having an intelligent conversation for once now you're taking it all the wrong way."

"Am I ma? Am I really?"

"Yes Malika! You are! I don't love my patients, yet I am very fond of some of them because they have been my patients for so long. I am trying to help them work through their issues. Why can't you understand that?"

"I can understand you helping, but there are two of your patients who are crazy."

"I know, I know... and I am trying to help them."

"How can you help them ma, when they can't even see what's happening to them?

"But what if it's too late?"

"Too late for what?" Malika had a look of shame in her eyes because she knew that what she had planned for her mother wasn't what she really wanted to do, but she felt like it was the only way to get her point across and finally be heard.

"What is it Malika, you do know you can talk to me?"

"Ma... there is something I have to tell you I really don't think you are going to like it."

"What is it, Malika? Wait a minute, hold that thought for two seconds." Corrine could tell Malika didn't think she was interested in what she had to tell her, but she was. For the first time in a long time, Corrine and her daughter had finally established a dialogue. Her cell suddenly went off and it was Traci.

"What? Okay, hold on, I'll be right there! Calm down, Traci, I'm coming." Malika knew what that call meant. "Go ahead, Mother, I know."

"Malika, I have to go. Wait a minute, how about you come with me. Maybe we can finish this conversation on the way to the hospital."

"The hospital? What happened?"

"Something about Traci's little sister, but I couldn't tell because she was hysterical. So are you coming?"

"Ma, go take care of it, I'll be here when you get back. I remembered something I have to do."

"Are you sure?"

"Yes, I'm sure. Plus, I have something I need to do myself, so go ahead and keep me posted."

"I will. Malika, I love you we will work through this."

"Yeah ma, we will." Malika watched her mother grab her keys and storm out the door.

.

Down at the precinct...

"There's something about Brenda's rape and what happened to that little girl that doesn't make sense Mills." Raynar said as he sat down at his desk.

"I know what you mean. I got a call a few moments ago from Corrine asking questions about Trey Bashir. Now why would a woman of that caliber be asking questions about him? How does she even know him? But there's something about the open rape case with Brenda that brings me back to the case we did when I first started on the force. Mills replied.

"Remember? How could I ever forget the headlines from the front page of The Heights Journal News, *LOCAL PARENTS ABUSED THEIR DAUGHTERS*. This town was terrified and we never heard the end of it." Raynar said.

"Right, but whatever happened to the sisters? Weren't they sent to a foster home or something? Weren't there four girls?" Mills was scratching his head, trying to remember the case.

"Yes, there were four sisters. The aunt took them all in until she couldn't handle them anymore. Corrine is one of those sisters." Raynar replied.

But what does Corrine have to do with the rape case or what happened to that little girl? Man we still have a beat up woman that no one seems to want to talk about either. You think that Trey had something to do with this? Wait a minute, didn't you and Corrine have something going on back in the day?" Mills asked.

"Yea, but nothing to brag about. You must admit that it's a sick coincidence that both Brenda and Mary show up at the same hospital with serious injuries. Also, Corrine has a past. I never did make the connection with the girls though. However, Corrine did very well for herself. She wanted to come back to help the community and those girls specifically so I heard. I never understood her reasons why. She would've been something special had it not been for her sisters introducing her to drugs. The whole family is messed up." Raynar said.

"Family? So are you saying there's some relation between the Brenda, Mary and Trey?" Mills asked as he looked through the case file.

"Well, Mary is Corrine's older and as far as Brenda, not sure what connection Corrine has with her. I do know that Corrine's father was who we arrested in the case as our number one suspect for abusing her and her sisters, and I think a cousin too when they were little. But the girls would never testify, neither would his wife at the time. So we couldn't make anything stick. The case never really was closed and went dormant for years especially after their father died in prison. Never re-opened it." Raynar replied.

"So do we have a case with Trey or are we searching for someone else that could've raped Brenda and beat up Mary, oh and abused that little girl." Mills began closing up files on his desk.

"Oh, we have a case, I believe Trey raped abused that little girl. Not sure if he had anything to do with Brenda's rape though. My gut tells me that all of this is linked to Corrine's past and as far as Mary well her husband Al has been beating her for years. We can't hold him if she's not pressing charges. My gut tells me that there is something else we are not seeing here. Something isn't right with any of this...Let's get a warrant for Trey, tell Al he is free to go and I'm going to head back over to the hospital and see if I can make some sense of all of this."

VOICES IN THE DARK

Chapter 20
Night before Friday at the hospital...

It was chaos inside the emergency room. There were about a dozen patients waiting to be seen. The nurses at the nurses' station gathered like they were having a party. They didn't seem to be too concerned about the chaos going on inside the ER. Corrine walked in and began to look around for Traci, but she was nowhere to be found. She asked one of the nurses where she may be and the nurse responded with an answer that neither Corrine was expecting.

"Excuse me, I'm friends of Traci Johnson. She came in earlier with her baby sister. I got a call from her to meet her here. Can you please tell me where she is?" Corrine asked the nurse that was holding the clipboard behind the nurse's desk.

"Who are you looking for again, Miss? Traci Johnson I don't seem to have her here on my patient list."

"She must be here because she said her baby sister was brought in the ER. But Traci isn't the patient, Dominique is. I'm not sure if she was checked in, but she has to be here. Can you check again?" The nurse checked her sheet again as she kept looking up at Corrine and then back at her clipboard. The nurse kept flipping through her lists but didn't seem to be able to give Corrine the answer she was looking for.

"Miss, I don't see the name of the person who you are looking for."

"So are you telling me that there was no young child brought in here tonight?"

"Wait a minute. Now that I think about it there was a badly beaten, abused young girl brought in by her sister and she disappeared. She very well may still be in the emergency room waiting area. Try there. Is there anything else I can help you with?"

"Do you have a chapel?"

"Yes, of course, it's down the hall and to the left."

"Thank you…"

The OR…

"Doctor, her sister dropped her off. What should I tell her?"

"Do we know who did this to this child? I want a Social Worker here immediately. Also, call those detectives down here that asked about her earlier. Whoever did this, had a lot of hate for this little girl. I don't understand how people could do such a thing to an innocent child."

"Will she be okay?" the Nurse asked.

"It's too soon to tell, she's a very lucky to be alive." The doctor responded, shaking his head in disbelief.

"I'll inform her sister…"

Brenda's room…

"How is she?" Eva asked the attending nurse who was standing right outside of Brenda's room.

"She's sleeping right now. We gave her a sedative to get her through the night. She's been through a lot. Try not to wake her okay? We want her to remain calm."

Eva walked into the room, grabbed the chair by the door so she could watch her cousin sleeping. The nurse was right. Brenda had been through hell and back. Eva had fallen asleep in her chair when she awoke; Brenda was gone from her room. Eva woke up and ran out to the nurse's station to ask if anyone knew where Brenda had walked off.

"Nurse, where is my cousin? She's not in her room. How long was I asleep?" Eva was in a panic because she knew Brenda was still upset from earlier.

"I don't know ma'am, maybe an hour or so. But I didn't see her leave the room, are you sure?"

"Of course I'm sure, her bed is empty. Where could she have wandered off? Plus, I thought you said she was heavily sedated?"

"Miss, she was. We made sure she swallowed her pill."

"Well, you didn't make sure she did a good job she is somewhere in this hospital or worse... she left the hospital again." Eva and the Nurses split up to comb the hospital to look for Brenda. They were going to every room on the floor.

The Chapel...

"Lord, I come to you this evening to beg for your forgiveness. Please help me to understand what has happened to the girls. I don't know how to help them. I want to help them so bad, but my fear is that she may be beyond help. Please help me to help them. I don't know what to do..." Corrine was sitting in the first row of the chapel with her head bowed down and tears flowing from her face.

"Well, you help them by admitting to them what you've done. Isn't that right?" A male's voice spoke from the back of the room. Corrine looked up and noticed Detective Raynar standing there wondered if he had heard her prayer.

"What are you doing here? Aren't you supposed to be out looking for the person raped Brenda and more importantly abused Traci's little sister. Corrine stood up and wiped the tears from her face with the tissue that Detective Raynar handed her.

"I got that handled and honestly, I think we both know who abused Dominique, don't we?" Corrine turned around and rolled her eyes at Detective Raynar forcing herself not smile from his presence. Detective Raynar and Corrine had a history from when they were younger. He was always in love with Corrine and always believed that he could save her from everything. "We do? Well if you know already Ray, what are you really doing here?"

"I'm here to help, Corrine. What do you think you're doing? At some point, these girls will figure this out like I did a few moments ago. It took me a minute to piece it all together, but I figured it out." Detective Raynar sat Corrine down and placed his arm around her. He wanted to let her know he was there for her.

"Corrine, you have to tell them. You can't keep counseling those girls and not tell them the truth. Those girls will figure it out what will you do when one of them decides to hurt you? Are you prepared for that? You're all alone in this quest. I heard that you were divorced now. I'm sorry."

"Thanks Ray, he was a jerk anyway I appreciate you wanting to help me Ray but I have to figure this out myself. We made a promise at least I kept my promise. But what Jackie and Mae did to those girls is unforgivable. There's no coming back from that. I also know that Eva's father was helping them. These girls are damaged need my help. I wished I knew what to do how to go about it." Corrine stood up and began to walk towards the front of the chapel to go check on Dominique.

"I understand, Corrine, but you know I'm here for you. You do know that, don't you? You don't have to do this alone. I know what you've been through. Please let me help you. I love you, Corrine."

"Ray please…. don't. I can't handle any more issues right now. I only came back to help the community and to help my…"

"Go ahead Corrine, say it. Can you even say it to yourself?"

Detective Raynar lifted Corrine's chin, wiped her tears from her face and kissed her as if he would never see her again. Corrine didn't hold back, she kissed him back and they held each other for what seemed to be hours. His soft lips and gentle hands made Corrine feel safe. She hadn't felt that way in a long time. She wanted Detective Raynar to take her away from all her past sins and pain. Corrine wanted all of this to go away. Hesitantly, Corrine's body gave in to his every touch until they were interrupted.

"Miss Castleberry you better come quick, your patient is going crazy in the waiting room." As Corrine, Detective Raynar the nurse approached the waiting room; they couldn't believe their eyes.

"Traci! What is the matter with you? Brenda!"

Traci and Brenda were fighting in the waiting room. Corrine tried to break it up, but she couldn't stop it. Detective Raynar got on the radio and called for his partner to come down to the hospital to help him. The nurse managed to get security up to the waiting room and they, along with Detective Raynar, managed to separate the women.

"This bitch started it! Miss C how could she know all my business! Did you tell her what we talked about?" Brenda asked as she was trying to catch her breath.

"She didn't have to tell me nothing, skank! I saw you in her office the same day I was there!"

Detective Raynar had a good grip on Traci, but she was trying hard to get her hands back to Brenda. Brenda had been taken away by security back to her room. Corrine started crying when she realized that the doctor who worked on Dominique had entered the room and by his facial expression the news wasn't good...

Jackie's apartment...

"Open the door! You have some nerve blaming me for your bullshit!"

"Hold on, I'm coming." Jackie shouted from behind the door. "Oh it's you... what the hell are you doing here? You got any money?"

"No, I don't have any money. You know the police brought me down to the station I'm sure they think I'm the one that beat you up. You better get your story straight because I had nothing to do with this."

"Oh please! Chill the fuck out! What's the matter? You don't want anybody to know what you've been doing in the hood, especially with all of us women? Does your wife know you here?" Jackie said as she laughed her way back into her living room to that dirty old chair.

"You don't worry about my wife. I can handle her. You need to handle your business. Don't be dragging me into none of this mess. Speaking of mess, where is your mate?"

Trey appeared from the back room with a beer in his hand. His pants were hanging halfway down to his butt he was high. He went and sat down next to Jackie and kissed her on the cheek. "You don't need to worry about me and my woman. We are doing fine, pops, but you shouldn't be in this neighborhood this late... you might not be able to leave. You know what I'm saying, ole man?" Trey let out a long sigh and blew weed smoke in his face as he spoke.

"Trey, you're nothing but a punk! Nothing but a local punk! Go talk that jive to someone who gives a shit. Look Jackie, it won't be long before the police come knocking at your door. For your sake, I hope you tell them the truth about what you did."

Trey stood up and lifted his shirt to show his .45 in his pants. "I don't think you want none of this, Gramps."

"Get the fuck out my house, Al! You have no right to talk to me like that. You're no better than me, screwing your own daughter Eva, marrying my sister Mary, and I know all about you Mary and beating up your ex-wife, my great aunt Linda! Yeah, I know all about it. So for your sake, you better hope I don't start singing like a canary. Now get out!" Jackie opened the door so Al could leave.

"Jackie, you will pay for this and unfortunately so will I."

Al walked out the door and headed over to Eva's house to see if he could catch her to apologize for his actions over the years. He wanted to come clean about everything, especially to her. But first, he needed to confess to his ex-wife Linda about his indiscretions.

VOICES IN THE DARK

Chapter 21
Revelations...

Al rushed back to Eva's place to clear his conscience. When Al rang the bell he found his ex wife Linda there instead and she wasn't happy.

"What are you doing here?"

"Linda, can I come in? We need to talk."

"Eva isn't here. And I don't want you here. Where is your wife Mary at? Shouldn't you be with her? I heard what you did to her. What you used to do to me. Oh Al, how could you..."Al sat down at the table with his wife and took her by the hand and tried to explain.

"We have nothing to talk about, Al. The detective called me and told me they want to question you about Mary. I already knew you would come by here to see if Eva was here. Well she isn't." Linda pulled back her hand from Al and slowly sipped her tea.

" I'm a sick man and I need help. I know that. But I never beat up that Mary or Jackie. I never touched neither of them. You have to believe me."

"Why should I believe you, Al? And what does Jackie have to do with this? You've been lying to me all these years. You think I don't know that you've been abusing Eva all these years and that her son may be your child? My own grandson is actually my stepson! I know all about you, Mae, Jackie Eva and what you did to Corrine. How could you deceive me all these years? I was stupid enough to stand by you in the beginning but when I found out about you and my own damn niece Mary, I had to put you out. But then you had to abuse our own daughter and impregnate her too? Not to mention, you've been creeping around here with Jackie for years and if Trey finds out the truth he'll kill you. Hell I should be the one to call him myself. I know what you and your brother did to Corrine as a little girl years ago when my mother died. I'm glad David died in prison and you should've been there with him. Do you remember that Al? I remember it like it was yesterday…"

Corrine's past
~June 13, 1981~
"C'mon here girl and stop all your fussing. She's gone now there's nothing you can do about it." Corrine's mother always spoke to her with coldness in her voice as if Corrine was a pain in her backside.

"How could you be so cold, Momma? Aren't you going to miss her, like me?"

Corrine asked. She couldn't understand why her mother didn't care about her very own mother being gone.

"Don't sass me girl! I loved her as much as she loved me. Does that answer your question?" her mother said.

Little Corrine along with her sisters was confused as to why their mother said she missed her, but looked so angry, yet happy because they buried Grandma.

They arrived back at the house where the family gathered to celebrate the life of Fannie Mae Johnson. Corrine saw family that she would only hear about as a little girl, but would never see in person. From uncles to aunts to distant cousins that Corrine only heard about when her mother was on the phone gossiping. Their house was a small three-bedroom shack with one bathroom. Her mother kept the spare room for company or if a relative dropped by and needed a place to sleep.

Corrine and her sisters were to serve everyone in the house. Especially Corrine because her grandmother, Fannie Mae taught her the most about serving. There were people everywhere in the house. Corrine's dad had retired to the back room in his recliner. He hated to mingle with his wife's mother's family, as much as they hated him. Corrine never understood why. As always, Corrine's mother would insist she help out in the kitchen, so she enlisted Corrine and her cousin Eva to start taking plates to the men in the house. This is how she learned to take care of a man and serve them; from her mother, and especially from grandma Fannie.

"Corrine, will you please bring these plates to your father and Uncle Al then take these plates to George and Bryan. When you are done, come back so I can give you more to hand out." her mother yelled from the kitchen.

"Coming, Ma," Corrine quickly responded.

Corrine's mother always felt like the women should serve the men first we were capable of serving ourselves. She would always say, "A woman's job is to serve the man of the house and ask no questions."

That's how she raised all her girls, but she gave special passes to Mae and Mary saying they weren't pretty enough to serve. It didn't help Corrine when her dad and uncle Al decided to test Corrine's knowledge of sex. Corrine had brought the plates of food to everyone but for some strange reason, her uncle Al and her dad kept asking for more, but only from Corrine. She didn't understand why they couldn't ask any of the other kids in *the house to bring them plates or her cousin Eva who also was handing out plates of food. Corrine didn't even get a chance to eat anything for all the walking around and serving she was doing.*

"Come here, Corrine, let Uncle Al get a good look at you. You've growing up so fast! I bet the boys can't leave you alone," he said, with a thirsty look on his face. Corrine's uncle Al was her daddy's baby brother. He grabbed her arm as she was setting up the plates of food on the fold up tray.

"Uncle Al, I am only nine. I don't like boys yet." Corrine responded jokingly. Corrine's dad glared at her as if she was doing something wrong. Corrine politely got up and walked out the room. She overheard them whispering to themselves about her how much she looked like her, but not her mom. Corrine always wondered who the "her" was that they were speaking of, but she never asked.

Al rubbed his hands together. "Brother, she is turning into a sweet tender little thing. Almost looks as sweet as…"

"Al! Watch your mouth! That's my little girl you're talking about. Don't make me beat your ass up in here." Corrine's father growled as he snatched Al up by the collar. Corrine's father looked as though he was going to punch Al in the mouth.

"I'm kidding, brother. I'm going to get me a beer, you want one?" Al was grinning from ear to ear, like the devil himself as Corrine's father let him go.

"Yeah, bring me two, so I don't have to get up again." Corrine's father slumped back into his favorite recliner with his hands folded across his belly.

"You got it."

Corrine's uncle Al never went to get the beer, instead he found little Corrine coming out the kitchen and followed her into the bathroom down the hall. Corrine thought he was going to turn in the other direction towards the living room where all the other adults were, but that never happened. Corrine went into the bathroom and when she turned around her Uncle Al was right behind her and had her cornered.

"Get out, Uncle Al! You're not supposed to be in here! Get out or I'm telling Momma." Corrine started to get upset and raise her voice to get her point across.

"Oh c'mon, Corrine, don't you love your Uncle Al? You know you're my favorite niece, right? Plus, your momma won't do anything anyway." Her uncle, Al, started licking his lips as he walked toward her and reached for her waist. He held his index finger on his lips, motioning her to be quiet.

"I'm not your only niece, Uncle Al! Go bother someone else. Get out of here so I can use the bathroom."

Corrine started to scream and pushed him towards the door, so he would get off of her. She was unsuccessful in all of her attempts. Al locked the door so little Corrine couldn't get out and wrestled her to the old porcelain tub where she chipped her front tooth. Al bent Corrine over, ripped her panties, and forced himself inside her tiny virgin walls from behind. He had such a strong grip on her mouth that her screams went unheard throughout the entire house. No one would hear her anyway with the stereo playing so loud all the people talking. Her screams and tears were lost.

"Uncle Al, stop it!" Corrine muffled as she tried to kick and wiggle her body from his grasp, but nothing was working.

Al abused Corrine from the back and had such a good grip on her little torso, that she felt her back pinch in pain. She kicked and screamed, but nothing Corrine did seemed to get her uncle off her. That's when Corrine heard the door bust open saw a glimpse of her mother's shoes. Corrine's mother stood there in silence and did nothing. She said nothing. She simply closed the door behind as if she was blinded by what she witnessed.

Corrine's uncle finished his business and left her lying on the bathroom floor, bruised, bloody and filled with shame. As her uncle zipped his pants, he whispered to her, "I knew you would be as sweet as your sister Jackie was."

Little Corrine slid down between the tub and the small sink and cried her little heart out. Corrine wasn't prepared for what was about to happen next. Corrine took what little strength she had left, grabbed the side of the tub pulled herself up. She turned on the water from the sink, grabbed the hand towel that hung right over the toilet seat and began to clean up. As she tried to wash the smell of her uncle off, Corrine's father entered the bathroom to her surprise her nightmare was about to begin all over again... from a different monster.

"Daddy, no! Please don't! What are you doing? I'm your daughter!"

Corrine's mouth started to hurt so bad from her chipped tooth, that she could barely get a good strong volume in her voice so someone could hear her cries. She was in so much shock and pain from what her uncle had done to her. Her panties were soiled and torn from her uncle's semen, that it made it *much easier for her father, who was ready to do his business. Corrine also knew that if she didn't be quiet and give in to her father's wishes, he'd beat her to a bloody pulp.*

"Shut up, Corrine! Keep quiet! This is punishment for what you did with my brother, your own fucking Uncle! You want to prance around here in front of him like a grown woman then you're gonna satisfy your daddy like a grown fucking woman. Now take me like you took him…"

Corrine's father violated her like her Uncle Al did. He sodomized little Corrine and ejaculated all over her caramel complexioned face. Corrine's parents were supposed to protect her; instead they punished and abused her. She could no longer cry about what her father did to her. This became a normal routine for Corrine and her father, until he started in on his other daughters. David continued this incestuous affair with his daughters until he was later arrested….

I didn't even believe my own daughter. How could you? I was so blind and didn't want to believe it! How could you abuse our daughter too?"

"Linda… I… I'm a very sick man and I need help."

"It's too late Al. It wouldn't be long before Corrine and that detective figured things out. Corrine came back to town to counsel people but also face her past and she'll figure it out. But I think Eva knows deep down inside you did something to her she also is aware that I know all about it. I should've protected my little girl... but I didn't."

"So what are you saying to me? What are you trying to say?"

Linda stood up and put her cup in the sink. Eva kept a set of carving knives in her kitchen right next to the sink. Linda grabbed the longest one she could find and turned around and lunged at Al with a promise. Al sat paralyzed with fear, but from the look in Linda's eyes, she meant business.

"I'm not saying, Al, this is a promise!! You need to check yourself into a facility for help and turn yourself in. In the meantime, stay far away from my daughter. If you don't, I promise you I will kill you where you stand. Do I make myself clear?"

Al pleaded for Linda to put the knife down and talk to him, but she wasn't trying to hear anything he had to say. "Al, do I make myself clear?" Linda stuck the point of the knife closer to Al's throat to make her point clear.

"Yes... you've made your point."

"Good! Now get the hell outta here before I kill you now."

"But Linda what will you do about Eva and Corrine? What will you tell the Detectives?"

"You don't worry about that. I will get her the help she needs. You stay the hell away from her, Al. Stay the hell away from me! Now get out!" Linda went into Eva's room and slammed the door.

Al stood there with a look of despair on his face. There was nothing he could do for his little girl now, nor Corrine. Al agreed with his Linda. The best thing was for him to leave and never return, but not before he made a long overdue phone call.

"Hello, this is Al Johnson. Yes, I know, it's been a long time. Yes, I can be there tonight." Al responded to the person on the other line. As Al walked out the door, he looked back at his Linda standing in her room doorway. He could see the years of pain on his her face as he shut the door behind him...

Back at the hospital...

"Sir? Brian, please get back into your bed. Nurse! Someone, please help me with this patient." The nurse pleaded for Brian to get back in his bed, but he was determined to walk right out the hospital. The nurse had asked Brian where he thought he was going. All he could manage to write was, "To find her. Bring her to me."

"Do you mean your wife? Shalae?" the nurse asked as she got him back into his bed.

"Yes," Brian nodded.

"Sir... I'm afraid that Shalae is not here. She left hours ago. She did leave a note for you at the nurse's station. I will bring it to you. But I need you to calm down and relax. Can you do that for me?"

Brian did what the nurse asked and got back into bed. He had pulled his IV out his arm so the nurse had to start a new drip. Once she got him comfortable in bed, she went to get his note for him along with something to eat. The nurse had brought in a plate from the food tray that was outside the room. It was Salisbury steak, corn, a stale piece of bread, a small bowl of Jell-O on the side a small helping of pudding.

Brian couldn't eat well his mouth was still sore, so the nurse had to mash up the food and feed him liquids intravenously. The cafeteria had mixed up the room orders. Brian was being cooperative because he hadn't eaten since the day before. As the nurse began to feed his IV, he motioned for her to hand him the note that Shalae left. Brian became enraged as he read it.

"Dear Brian,

I'm truly sorry for what I did to you. But this was the only way I could see myself out of this destructive relationship that we are both in. I was planning to tell you tonight at dinner, but as I warned you before…if you had hit me again it would be your last. Well playa, I'm pregnant. It's yours and you don't have to worry about anything. I don't need your drug money and I don't need you. I've been carrying you this whole time in this relationship I'm sick of it. So I really do hope you get better and I pray to God that you don't do this to another woman. Your consequences for abusing me could be a lot worse with a different woman.

I love you Brian, but I love me more. Take care of yourself
    Love,
    Shalae
    P.S. Please don't try to find me. If you do, that mysterious bag of cocaine will find its way to the cops along with the owner. Get your life together. Brian I wish you luck…

Brian crumbled up the letter and threw his food tray against the wall. The food spilled all over the floor and some even splattered the nurse's uniform.

"Sir! I guess it wasn't good news," the nurse said as she left to call for maintenance to clean up.

All he could do was sit there and look out the window and think about what he had done and now what he had lost in the process.

Chapter 22
Revelations II....

"Doug, is she okay?" Corrine asked.

"She will be okay, but she was badly abused. Someone raped this little girl over and over again. I called Social Services and they are on the way here now. Do you have any idea who would do this to her."

"Yes I do. At least I think I do. It's complicated. But I believe it was her own father that did this to her."

"Corinne what are you talking about? Where is the child's mother? To my understanding, she was brought in by her sister. Is this correct?"

"Yes. Is there some place we can go and talk so I can explain?"

"Yes, back in my office."

As Corrine and the doctor headed back to his office, she turned back to see where Traci was and to make sure she was safe. Brenda was safe with Detective Raynor. Corrine had motioned for Ray to sit with her and she should be right back.

Raynar knew exactly what Corrine meant. "Don't worry, Corrine, I have her. Please come back to me... please." Corrine motioned to him nodding her head yes as she walked down the hallway with the Doctor.

As Corrine and the doctor headed to his office, all she could think to herself was how she could save the girls from total destruction.

"So Corrine, explain to me what's going on?"

Corrine sat down and clutched her hands together to find the strength to begin to explain this destruction that had taken place. "I really don't know where to begin. Will Dominique recover from her wounds?"

"Well she'll recover, but she is badly bruised and scarred. I'm more worried about her state of mind. If you know who did this, I do have to report it. You do know this Corrine, don't you?"

"Yes I do... but hear me out for a second, okay?"

"Okay Corrine, enlighten me."

"Well, one of my patients, Brenda, is a sick woman. She was attacked a few weeks ago. But when she was attacked it did something to her. Something in her changed. The irony is... the young lady that Brenda was fighting is her sister and they are my daughters..." Corrine said as she let out a long sigh of relief.

"Are you serious Corrine?" Doug stood speechless.

"I know but no one knew. I used drugs real heavy back then and I was prostituting. My sister, Jackie and her boyfriend Trey were my suppliers, but they weren't into it as bad as they are now. My other sister Mae took my first-born Brenda, Jackie took my youngest Traci and Mary took my middle child Shalae. I thought I could trust them with my daughters that I couldn't take care of. I was so wrong to think I could keep this secret for so many years. But my daughters were being abused by my sisters and my uncle, the same way we were abused as kids growing up."

"Do they know that you might be their mother? Wait a minute, who is the father because we…"

"I do. But they all think they have a different mother. My sisters were supposed to care for them, but I can see clearly they both failed at the job for me. Brenda changes every time I see her. I also have to protect my youngest daughter, Malika, from all of this. Doug, I don't know who the daddy is at this time. You know how bad I was, remember?"

"I remember. I do. But I also know that you and I… well we used to have a good time, you know? So let me get this straight, you left your daughters with your sisters they abused them all their life, is that right?" Doug had placed his hand on Corrine's shoulder to console her.

"Yes, they did. So I relocated back here to help. But I think my daughters and my sisters are beyond help at this point."

"So what do you need from me? I want to help you any way I can. You know we go way back, so I'm here for you. You know this, at least I hope you do."

"Thanks, Doug. I appreciate that. Well, I meet with the girls tomorrow in our last therapy session. I had the two of them write journals to their mother about what they wanted to say that's when I will tell my daughters the truth. I need you to keep an eye on Dominique for me, please. Don't let her sister Traci… my daughter… take her anywhere."

"You got it, Corrine. You have my word."

"Thanks, Doug."

"You are welcome, Corrine. Oh please be careful we can discuss the matter of paternity when you are ready to do so."

"I'm gonna try. Thank you."

Corrine left the doctor's office feeling a bit relieved that she had finally told someone part of her secret. The reason why she was called back to her community was to save her daughters that she failed so many years ago. As Corrine approached the emergency room, she noticed that Detective Raynar was still there with Traci. Traci had drifted off to sleep in the chair.

"Are you okay Corrine?" Detective Raynar asked?

"Yes. It's time. It's time they all knew the truth. Thank you for being here for me."

"Anytime, Corrine, but we need to close this case. Call me and let me know what's going on."

"I will, Ray. You'll have all the answers to close your case tomorrow... I promise."

Brenda's room...

"Brenda! We have been looking everywhere for you. What were you thinking leaving your room again?" Eva asked Brenda as she helped her back into bed.

"Eva, I went to the bathroom and some girl accused me of some things and we ended up fighting. I don't even know this girl."

"What girl? Fighting? Brenda you're a little too old to be fighting, don't you think?" Eva said as she pulled the sheet and blanket over Brenda.

"You're right, Eva. But some girl who apparently recognized me, but I don't know her, pushed me when I was coming out the bathroom. Apparently, we are seeing the same therapist, Miss Castleberry. But there was something about her eyes that were very familiar to me."

"Brenda, I'm going to need you to take it easy and relax."

"You think I'm making this up, Eva?"

Brenda I don't know. You've been disappearing a lot lately you don't even remember. Something is definitely going on with you. I wish we both knew what it was."

"Eva, speaking of which, there's something I need to ask you. I don't know how to ask you this so I'm going to put it out there."

"Oh c'mon cousin, you can ask me anything."

"Okay... your dad raped you, didn't he? He raped the both of us, didn't he? You can tell me the truth, Eva. Please..."

Eva stood motionless and didn't know how to respond to Brenda's question. She wasn't sure if this was the right time to go into this or not. But Eva knew she had to give Brenda an answer.

Chapter 23
Friday…

It was Friday morning and Brenda wasn't feeling herself today. She kept wondering if she was going crazy. So many things weren't making sense. She knew her father had abused her and she believed that he had abused Eva as well. *Was he the man in my dreams?* Brenda thought. But there was something about the girl's eyes that Brenda couldn't shake out of her mind. She couldn't help but to wonder if she knew the girl from somewhere, but she couldn't think where.

"Brenda? Brenda Johnson?" the nurse asked as she came to give Brenda her check out papers.

"Yes, I am Brenda Johnson. Are you here to release me?"

"Yes I am. My name is Nurse Nichols we need to go over some details before the doctor releases you today."

Brenda wasn't interested in being checked out that meant she had to go home and face her issues. All she could think about was the girl who had accused her of such childish things. Why was she having dreams of some man doing something to her? Did they catch the guy that did this to her? Was she really going crazy why is her mother never there for her?

As Brenda answered the questions for the nurse, Corrine walked in with Detective Raynar. "Hi Brenda, how are you feeling today? You remember Detective Raynar, don't you?" Corrine asked as she walked around to the left side of Brenda's bed to talk to her.

"Yes, I remember him, I think. What are you both doing here? I thought my cousin was coming for me?" Brenda had asked as she sat upright in the bed to speak to the Detective.

"Brenda, we need to talk to you about the night you were raped. Can we do that? I know it may be painful for you," Detective Raynar asked as he pulled out his little pocket notebook and pen.

"Look, like I told the good doctor, I wasn't raped. Dr. Castleberry, why are you doing this to me? My cousin brought me back here saying that I needed to be officially checked out by the doctor. That's the only reason why I came back. But you consistently keep pushing some rape thing on me. Why?" Brenda said angrily as she folded her arms and looked past Corrine and starred out her room window.

"Brenda, please. Let us help you. You had a traumatic event happen to you we think we know who did this to you, but we need to ask you some questions. So can you please try, for me... please?" Corrine pleaded with Brenda as she held her hand to give her some moral support.

"Why don't you go help that bitch that attacked me in the emergency room? I was going to the bathroom and she went into a complete rage and came at me. Like my cousin said, I'm no spring chicken, but that bitch deserves her ass whooped. So go help her, I don't need you."

"Brenda, you do need us as far as that girl goes, there's something you should know about her..." Corrine took a long deep breath and looked over at Detective Raynar before she spoke. He nodded, as if to agree with what she was about to say.

"Brenda, you and Traci are sisters..." Corrine stepped back to give Brenda a moment to take in what had she said. Brenda sat up further and continued to look out the window as if she didn't hear anything Corrine said. All of a sudden, the tears started to pour down Brenda's face.

"Miss C, exactly what are you telling me? Are you saying that my mother has another child that I know nothing about? Is that what you're saying to me right now?"

"What I am trying to say Brenda is that you and Traci have the same mother, but your mother isn't your mother. She raised you at my request."

"Excuse me, Miss C! What you say to me? Are you crazy, coming in my room with this madness? Get out! Take your handyman with you! Both of you get out!" Brenda demanded as she pulled the covers over her face and began to cry like a little baby.

"Brenda, can you please hear me out?" Corrine begged Brenda to hear her side of the story.

"Hear your side? You've been lying to me all this time while you were treating me. You never said anything you knew I wanted my mother's love all this time you mean to tell me you knew something about my childhood and you kept me from it? Get the hell out! Get out now!" Brenda threw the glass vase of flowers sitting next to her at Corrine and the Detective. Detective Raynar pulled Corrine by the arm and began to walk out the room. All Corrine could do was look back at Brenda and come to grips with the reality of the damage that had been done.

"Corrine, she's not stable enough to handle the truth, not all of the truth right now. Give her some time."

"Ray, we don't have time. She's a walking time bomb if I don't come clean and fix this, I'm afraid that she'll do something to someone or worse... herself."

As Corrine and Detective Raynar started to walk out, Eva was coming up the hallway with Brenda's mother. Corrine had no idea she would run into her sister, nor did she ever want to have this conversation. But Corrine felt desperate had to do something to save the girls.

"I swear before God himself, if you ever lay a hand on my daughter again, not even Jesus himself will be able to save you. Do you hear me?" Corrine screamed at Mae as she walked inside Brenda's room with Eva.

"Auntie, what is this woman talking about? Who is this woman?" Eva asked Mae who stood there with a blank face as if she'd seen a ghost.

"You were supposed to stay away. Why the fuck did you come back here anyway? Brenda would be fine if you didn't go meddling into her life. Corrine you're nothing but trouble! You always were. You should be thanking me!" Mae was furious at Corrine's presence.

"I told you one day I would be back. You're going to pay for what you and that no good sister of ours did to me and as well as my daughters! I swear it. With every breath in my body, you will pay for what you did!" Detective Raynar had to drag Corrine out of the hospital because the look she gave her sister was if she was going to kill her right where she stood.

"Auntie Mae, who was that woman?" Eva asked.

Mae looked at Eva with a look of sadness. It was her sister and she was right. She hadn't done right by Brenda growing up it was time she corrected that once and for all. Mae and Eva walked into Brenda's room. Brenda was sobbing uncontrollably under her blanket, trying to hide her tears of pain from the world.

"Brenda, what's wrong? Did that therapist upset you?" Eva asked as she sat down next to Brenda's bed.

Brenda pulled the blanket from over her face and sat straight up in her bed. Brenda was trying to take everything in about what was presented to her by Miss Castleberry and Detective Raynar. Brenda stared at her so-called mother, waiting for her to give her an answer, but it never came. Mae never even looked at her direction because deep down inside she knew she was wrong.

"Don't you have something to say to me? Well don't you?" Brenda asked her mother who sat there in silence.

"What do you want me to say, Brenda? I'm sure she told you everything. All the gory details about our family's past and what she thinks we did to you. I've been nothing more than a good mother to your sorry ass. You should be grateful anyone wanted you."

"You bitch!" Brenda jumped out of bed and lunged at her mother. She hit her in the head with her bed pan and continuously beat her mother in her head."

"Brenda, stop it, you're killing her! Stop it Brenda!" Eva shouted as she tried to grab Brenda from off of her Aunt.

Brenda sat on top of her mother, beating her in the head over and over. "I hate you! I hate you! I hate you!" The blood started to gush out of Brenda's mother's head as Brenda pounded her head onto the hospital room floor.

"Someone please help me, she's killing her! Please help me!" Eva screamed as she ran down the hallway to grab the nearest nurse.

All the nurses rushed to the room and pulled Brenda off her unconscious mother. One of the nurses called for the doctor on call a gurney for her mother.

"Let her die! Let her die! Don't help her!" Brenda said in a calm tone as she sat on the edge of her bed with a bloody bedpan in her hands.

"Brenda, what the hell has gotten into you? How could you say that about your own mother? What did she ever do to you that was so bad you had to beat her like that?"

Brenda slid back on her bed and stared down at her bloody hands. She couldn't believe what she had done, but it felt good to her. For years, she held in so much anger towards her mother now that the truth was out, Brenda felt ified by her actions. It's almost as if Brenda had become another person right before Eva's eyes.

"Are you going to answer me Brenda? Brenda!" Eva kept calling Brenda's name until she answered her.

"My name isn't Brenda, it's Nina and that woman was never my mother..."

Chapter 24
The truth… six months later

"Hi Ray, no she seems to be okay, thanks for asking. How about we meet up later today at my office? Good, see you then." Corrine closed her phone and placed it on the passenger seat beside her. She turned the ignition off, put her keys inside her bag and sat. Exhaling, she knew it was time she faced the truth about everything that had taken place over the last few weeks. It was time the girls knew the truth about her. Realizing all the pain she may have caused by returning home, there was really only one way to save her daughters. Corrine couldn't abandon them again, so she decided to stay in town, so she could keep them safe and sane from themselves. So much damage had been done though their life went back to normal she still feared for her and Malika's life.

Brenda was placed in a mental facility thirty minutes away from Corrine's office. She had set it up with a former colleague of hers who works at the facility to be able to visit her regularly and monitor her behaviors. At this point, Brenda's alternate personalities had not surfaced in six months. Brenda was able to control the dominant one, Nina and as long as she was medicated her alter never resurfaced. Corrine was able to get Shalae out of her abusive relationship and relocate her and her unborn child to another city. Though she was never able to tell Shalae the truth, she knew one day she would get her chance. Corrine and Malika's life went back to normal and Jackie, Trey and Al were serving time for the beating of Mary and the molestation of Dominique. Aunt Linda was still holding strong but stayed to herself. Corrine visited her from time to time. Mae and Corrine never spoke again.

Corrine gathered her things to go inside and visit with Brenda. Today would've been six months since they'd last seen each other. Corrine locked her car door, looked both ways headed into the facility.

"Good Morning, Dr. Castleberry."

"Good Morning, Geneva. How are you today?"

"I'm fine. You're here to see your daughter, right?"

"Yes. How is she today?"

"Quiet."

"Well, that's good. Have a good day Geneva."

"You too Doctor."

Corrine entered her security clearance code and walked through the double glass doors. As Corrine approached the elevator, she pushed the up button a mysterious young woman came and stood beside Corrine. Corrine looked at the woman, smiled asked if she was going up or down to the basement.

"No, I am going up," the woman responded.

"Okay," Corrine replied, "Up it is. Do you have a family member here?" Corrine continued to pry, firing questions at the mysterious woman who was dressed in black and wore a black veil. Corrine thought this was weird, but then compared to the types of patients that Corrine came across, this was normal. The woman never responded to Corrine's line of questions, but she did follow her off the elevator onto the same floor.

"Hey Dr. Castleberry," the nurses said from behind the nurses station.

"Morning ladies." Corrine had started to open the room door to Brenda's room when she turned around and was face to face with the mysterious woman in black. "Eva, what are you doing here? I had no idea you were visiting Brenda today?"

"I'm not, I came to see you."

Startled and confused, Corrine didn't understand what Eva was talking about why Eva was dressed in black and disguising her face. "Why me, Eva?" Brenda responded.

"You failed to come back for me too. You don't deserve to live..."

Corrine's blood began to gush out slowly from her mouth and glide down the side of her face. The force from the knife was too much for Corrine to bear. Shock took over her body and she could not let out a whimper as Eva dug deeper into Corrine's heart, deeper and deeper, until Corrine fell backwards into Brenda's room.

Sitting quietly in her chair, staring out the window, Brenda smiled as she extended her hand out for her cousin.

Eva walked over to Corrine as the nurses came rushing to her aide.

"What did you do? Somebody call the police please! Dr. Castleberry has been hurt badly!" one of the nurses motioned for someone to get help as she tried to pick up Corrine's head. "Hold on Dr. Castleberry, help is coming, help is coming..."

Eva grabbed Brenda's hand, kneeled down like a child and placed her head in Brenda's lap as they both gazed out the window without uttering any words between them.

"I told you, Brenda, I'll always protect you. Now you're safe…"

A note from the Author...

Abuse comes in many forms; physical abuse, mental, emotional and sexual abuse. If you know someone who is being abused please tell someone or report it to your local police department. Telling someone is the first step to saving a life.

When you choose to speak up, you disable the abuser's power over you. Always remember you are worth of love, joy, peace and comfort. We were all meant to love and to be loved. So speak up!

SPEAKING UP BREAKS THE CYCLE.

Continue to break the cycles of abuse. Keep talking. Keep telling and most of all know that you are worth it!

EBONI CHASE

WEBSITES:

WWW.RAINN.COM

WWW.CHILDHELP.ORG

WWW.VICTIMSOFCRIME.ORG

WWW.THEHOTLINE.ORG

WWW.NNEDV.ORG

WWW.NATIONALCHILDRENSALLIANCE.ORG

WWW.CHILDHELP.ORG

www.ingramcontent.com/pod-product-compliance
Lightning Source LLC
Chambersburg PA
CBHW071151170626
46809CB00002B/856